INFERNO OF SILENCE

It was a pleasure to meet you at Tynemouth Market.

by

Tolu' A. Akinyemi

First published in Great Britain as a softback original in 2020

Copyright © Tolu' A. Akinyemi
The moral right of the author has been asserted.
All rights reserved.

No part of this publication may be reproduced, stored in a retrieval system, or transmitted, in any form or by any means, without the prior permission in writing of the author, nor be otherwise circulated in any form of binding or cover other than that in which it is published and without a similar condition including this condition being imposed on the subsequent purchaser.

Typesetting by Word2Kindle

Cover Design by Rewrite Agency

Published by 'The Roaring Lion Newcastle'

ISBN: 978-1-913636-02-9

Email:
tolu@toluakinyemi.com
author@tolutoludo.com

Website:
www.toluakinyemi.com
www.tolutoludo.com

ALSO, BY Tolu' A. Akinyemi from 'The Roaring Lion Newcastle'

"Dead Lions Don't Roar" (A collection of Poetic Wisdom for the Discerning Series 1)

"Unravel your Hidden Gems" (A collection of Inspirational and Motivational Essays)

"Dead Dogs Don't Bark" (A collection of Poetic Wisdom for the Discerning Series 2)

"Dead Cats Don't Meow" (A collection of Poetic Wisdom for the Discerning Series 3)

Never Play Games with the Devil (A Collection of Poems)

A Booktiful Love (A collection of Poems)

DEDICATION

To the memory of my late grandmother, "Mama Christianah Olaosebikan Akinleye (Mama Alaanu). Thank you for birthing the flames of storytelling within me. I miss you now and always."

And to your daughter, my lovely and affable Sweet Mother—Temidayo Akinyemi, I wouldn't trade you for silver or gold.

CONTENTS

Dedication v
Acknowledgements ix

Black Lives Matter. 1
In the Trap of Seers 29
Everybody don Kolomental 63
Inferno of Silence. 85
Return Journey. 113
Trouble in Umudike. 161
Blinded by Silence 179

Bio 197
Author's Note. 201

ACKNOWLEDGEMENTS

Special appreciation to *Abigail's* Baby and my *Ololufe "Olabisi."* Thanks for listening to my stories and providing great critique and feedback.

Shout out to my number block and book craving children, Isaac and Abigail. Thanks for feeding my creative energy with some nice lexicons at a time I needed it. I have the best kids any father could wish for, and I am proud of you amazing ones.

To my ever-supportive and selfless parents, Gabriel and Temidayo Akinyemi. Thanks for the support throughout the years. I cherish you both more than words can express.

Special thanks to my editors, Gabrielina Gabriel Abhiele and Jennie Rosenblum, for being a vital part of this new phase as I metamorphose from a poet and essayist to a storyteller. It's been a joy working with you both on this booktiful journey.

To Omotayo Sangofadeji, my one and only "Omomenteeor", my booktiful friend and creative gang member. Thanks for the critique, feedback and giving me the nudge, I am on the right path as I share these words with the World. It's been a joy sharing those stages with you and watching you grow in leaps and bounds. The future is ours to conquer. And sincere appreciation to your lover "Adedotun" for re-activating our famous loan system.

A final thanks to everyone who has supported me on this journey that keeps unraveling so many booktiful experiences.

BLACK LIVES MATTER

BOOM! BOOM!

Every ball blast into the net sounded like gunshots reverberating in the atmosphere. For a moment, as the crowd celebrated Igbobi Stars' second goal, I saw a flash of myself seated among them in a wheelchair weeping for my team, Shoot for the Stars. The late Uzochukwu Emefiele, who had long been buried, was on the touchline barking orders at us. The riotous thoughts made me frail, and my dazzling form on the football pitch was now a distant memory. I continued to crisscross the realm of hallucination and trauma intermittently.

"Ikemefuna, pass me the ball!" one of my team members yelled, jolting me from the manic thoughts playing ping pong in my head. I did but with less enthusiasm which continued till the 90th minute. We lost the match by four goals to nil. The supporters of the winning team chanted the song, *Oleh Oleh Oleh Oleh*. It felt like mockery to me. I had never been this dismayed because of a loss. I looked around the crowd searching for nothing in particular, beads of sweat gathering on my forehead. Behind me was a group of youths clamouring for an autograph. I barely noticed them until a young couple at a distance, staring at me with disappointing gazes, caught my attention. I tried to pull myself together to fake a smile as I turned to face them, but my countenance betrayed my efforts. I could see their enthusiasm drop. Petrified, they walked off, one after the other. As I watched my disappointed fans walk away from me, I couldn't blame them.

"I'm s-o-rr-y," I tried to utter but the phrase ended up in whispers. It wasn't me. It was my confidence that I was starting to lose in the club, a club I once loved and adored.

I wore the jerseys of some of my favorite players in Shoot for the Stars, Ibadan, long before I was signed onto the team. It was my boyhood club. Dad and Mom supported my dreams of being a footballer steadfastly with every dime and sweat until the day a fatal accident claimed their lives.

"Blacky will make us proud, someday," Dad and his friends used to say when they watched me play in the community field during our locally organized football matches.

"Blacky has long legs like Kanu Nwankwo," another would remark. They called me Blacky each time my striking skills amazed and impressed them. Other times, I remained Ikemefuna. My dad often teased my mom that I was this dark in complexion because she drank too much black coffee while pregnant and burned my skin in the process.

I liked the feel of the little stardom I experienced, so, each day, I yearned for more. I wanted to be a name to reckon with for the sake of fame and nothing else. I wanted to fill my garage and that of my parents with the latest automobiles and cause traffic with my convoy wherever I went. I wanted to be a viable brand with worldwide appeal.

I thought being a player for Shoot for the Stars was my biggest dream come true. But with every actualisation of a dream comes a bigger dream to be actualised. Until then, I painted smiles on the faces of our club supporters with my artistic skills. I painted dreams of what's possible for the next generation. The CAF Champions League became a plaything. The trophy cabinet was brimming with an array of honours. Whenever I walked through the streets of Ibadan, an army of supporters would throng me. Seeing teenagers, barefoot, kicking tattered leather balls amongst the crowd always made me surge with emotions. My name sold shirts and match day tickets in the league. I was the 'star' in the name Shoot for the Stars. I had always ***shot*** for the stars even if I had, a number of times, landed amongst thorns and rocks.

The match with Igbobi Stars was an example of landing among rocks. The four consecutive abysmal displays and disjointed performances on the pitch after that were more terrible landings which led to the drastic decision I made that changed the course of my life and aspirations.

I requested a meeting with the chairman, Ogbeni Kosoko, in his office. Hung on his wall was a wooden frame with the inscription, "We are the shooting stars; we shoot for the stars." That inscription was far from the current reality after the tragic events that rocked the foundations of the club. We had become the shooting shadows or more aptly, the shooting basket.

My countenance contradicted the chairman's warm reception and smile as I took a seat opposite him. *You must be mistaken if you think I'm here to discuss the way forward with the team*, I thought sarcastically.

"My boy, hope you're coping well in these trying times?" he asked, still smiling. I managed to mumble a lousy, "Yes, Sir."

"I understand your concerns for Shoot for the Stars. In fact, any suggestions from you would be gladly welcome."

My thoughts were confirmed. I shook my head and chuckled from within. The chairman could sense something was wrong, but before he could ask further, I blurted out courageously, even though I was fidgeting, "I want to leave. I want to leave Shoot for the Stars football club." It had taken me a while to muster the courage to tell him.

The welcoming smile on the chairman's face suddenly disappeared. "Don't abandon us during our trying times," he retorted with a look of self-pity serenading his face.

"I can't play here again sir, not just for Shoot for the Stars but in this country."

The chairman emerged from his seat and began pacing up and down his office. I bowed my head and fixed my gaze on the marble floor. I was a bit nervous about what he would say next. After a moment of deep introspection, Ogbeni Kosoko said, "I can't hold you down. If you want to ply your trade in a foreign league, you have my blessings," nodding his head in affirmation.

The next morning, as I stepped out of the bathroom and turned on the television, a reporter was on air announcing that I had been granted a transfer to play outside Nigeria. I watched as people gave their opinions as to why I had chosen to leave. My mind raced back to the scene of the accident.

Uzochukwu Emefiele's body lying lifeless on the bumpy road under the dark sky had never ceased to recur in my head. Since the day I saw him slaughtered like a chicken, I believed that one day, unless I took a new route, I would end up like him. Lifeless, too. That night, the team and I were on an away trip to Enyinnaya football club in Aba. I remember politely scolding the driver, Ogbonna, as he gulped several spirits and Paraga just before the trip.

"It gives me the drive to drive on," he joked poetically, widening his eyes for me to see the 'positive' effect the spirits and Paraga had on him.

The coaster bus we were traveling in was stopped at over ten police checkpoints, but the police were more interested in the chant, "Anything for the boys" and with loud voices, wished us a safe journey, faces brimming with delight. The last police checkpoint we encountered was at Benin-Ore road before the trip became a harvest of confusion, blood and tears. As was the custom, the policeman who led the line looked left and right before locking hands with Ogbonna's to receive some rumpled notes. I could see the police officers through the side-view mirror hurriedly scurrying away as if oblivious of impending danger.

As the night progressed, my teammates and I started to fall asleep. Sounds of yawns, throats clearing and snores were heard here and there. Ogbonna hummed a famous Yoruba drunkard song as he swerved from left to right.

"Guy, abeg reduce your voice," Aliyu warned with a sleepy voice.

Suddenly, we heard a loud bang. Ogbonna had driven us into a pothole, and a tyre had forcefully pulled out. The bus swirled and crashed on its side, hitting an orange seller and a tyre repair merchant by the roadside. We were alarmed from our slumber by the chaos and began tossing our heads from side to side, trying to figure out what just happened as we groped in the dark, narrow bus. Someone managed to reach out to Aliyu, who groaned in pain from a corner. He had broken his bones and couldn't move. We managed to squeeze ourselves out of the now rickety bus along with him. But not all of us came out alive. Some had died instantly as their heads smashed against the windscreen with a thud while their eyes were still shut.

Boom! Boom! Boom!

We heard gunshots in the air. All of us fell to the ground to dodge the bullets fired into the atmosphere. But for Uzochukwu Emefiele, it wasn't a dodge; a bullet had hit him. My eyes went wet in an instant as I saw blood pour from the flesh of the team's assistant coach while he struggled for survival. From afar, I saw a group of armed men in black tee shirts, trousers and bandanas approach us. My limbs went numb immediately. An obese man the gang members called *Kapon* emerged from their midst barking orders at us. He bore semblance to the ringleader of the gang. I stole a quick glance and all I saw was a man who looked hardened, with unkempt hair and his lips darkened from what I deemed to be excessive use of marijuana. I tried to steal a second glance, but the butt of the gun to my head sent me into panic, shaking like a fish desperate for water. It made me realise that I had to obey Kapon's orders to the letter if I stood a chance at surviving my ordeal.

Kapon raised his gun and fired continuously again as the gang had done earlier. His fingers were excessively flippant, pulling the trigger mistakenly at Uzochukwu Emefiele, finally ending his life. Laughing in hysterics, Kapon shouted, "I love the smell of blood!" Some of the gang members searched us, taking away our money and valuables while others searched the bus which was now looking tightly squeezed. When they were done, they dispatched. This time, the police were nowhere to be found.

Half an hour after the robbery, mean looking police officers adorned in shirts with the inscription 'Federal SARS' arrived at the scene barking, "Where are they? Where are they?" They swayed from side to side, jumping up and down like amateurs in a war scene. When they could not get hold of any suspect, they chose their own suspect- Ogbonna, the driver. He looked back at us pleadingly as he was thrown into their van in handcuffs. I doubted if I would ever see Ogbonna's colourful smile again. While I blamed him for carelessness in my heart, I didn't wish him an arrest.

The premier league gave us three weeks to mourn our dead. The State Commissioner of Police paid his condolence visit to the training ground and was received by the club chairman. He wore the old black uniform that had now been shelved by the police force. I thought that wasn't out of place as he was here to mourn and drink from the cup of overflowing grief. CP Olagunju, voiced with authority, "I promise you all that we will get to the root of this matter." I sat on a brown stool, visibly shaken and shaking my head in disdain as the CP's words sounded empty. I could tell he was in his usual mood- deliver half-hearted promises that looked insurmountable. The unresolved murder mysteries in the state continues to taint his once lofty achievements in the police force. Upon delivering his speech, he left through the backdoor.

The skies turned dark, blood flowed freely, dreams shattered, and families were mourning. My eyes had become sore from crying and my hands, numb. The last time I had this type of numbing sensation was the day I watched my father and mother lowered six feet under the ground. I wished the club could afford me therapy so I could overcome the trauma quickly. Up until the disgraceful match with the Igbobi Club and the other matches that followed, every goal sounded like a gunshot and every cheer from the crowd sounded like the voices of Kapon and his gang.

Two weeks after my meeting with him, the chairman grudgingly accepted the best bid out of the three bids received from foreign clubs, following a fierce scramble for my signature. My parents were gone and my relatives were scattered far and wide, so,

I wrote letters to a few people I thought I could call blood before sojourning into the Whiteman's land. First, I started with "Dear..." but there was really nothing dear about the people I was writing to except that we had the same ancestors. I like to take the bull by the horn, so I simply stated their full names at the salutation.

Will money grow on trees? Will the ghost and trauma of the last few weeks be buried? Only time will tell, I thought as I sealed each envelope with the saliva on my tongue.

The chairman offered to drive me to the airport on the day of my departure. He had always been drawn to me. In fact, I'm still amazed at the ease with which he let me leave Shoot for the Stars. Just before I boarded, he placed the palm of his hand on my shoulder and said to me, "Go well. Make us proud." I thought I heard something like a shaky voice as he said those words. I didn't bother finding out. I placed my palm on the back of his hand, which was still resting on my shoulder and smiled.

"I will, Sir," I replied to him.

He watched me mount each step until I was inside the plane. For a minute, I hallucinated the face of my father watching me walk into the plane.

The take-off was announced a few minutes after I was settled. Looking out the window, I felt loneliness within even though the chairman had tried to ease me of the feeling by seeing me off to the airport. Although I was happy to be embarking on a new course in my life, I felt a strange cold surge within me as I couldn't envisage what awaited me.

I hoped that playing in a foreign league would boost my chances of playing for the national team by a mile. With all my artistry, skills and trophy honours on the football pitch, the national team coaches avoided selecting the best players in the local league like a plague. They would first select the top performing players who played abroad before selecting other players who frequently kept the benches in their football club warm. Those of us who played in the domestic league were treated like unwanted groceries past their sell by date, dumped on a shelf. The rumour mill was rife with news that selection of these players resulted from underhand dealings which are only whispered in hushed tones. So, I awaited the next national team selection with bated breath.

My first step on the European soil felt like a step on gold dust but the feeling of ecstasy soon faded away a few days after. Walking through the city centre, I was held captive by eyes that looked as if they were falling out of their sockets. Some of those faces looked colourless, devoid of a smile. I turned around me in a bid to figure out what went wrong. When I couldn't find an answer, I stole into a convenience in a restaurant to take a proper look at myself in the mirror. I bent my head over, turned around, and checked my sides to see if something was hidden in me that made me stink or sting. I found none. I repeated the same actions over and over again until I was certain I had seen nothing. *I have to figure this out*, I thought aloud while walking through the door of the convenience. Someone chuckled from behind. I turned around to see an Indian bearded man in white robe. He clasped his hands together and took a bow, smiling lightly.

"Hi," I said in response to what I guessed was his method of greeting.

First, he started off in Hindu which got me thinking he was somewhat deranged mentally. But then, he continued in English. "You're new here brother?"

"Umm… Sort of," I replied, not sure if it was safe to inform a stranger of my recent immigration status. Back in Nigeria, we were expected to not act like *Johnny Just Comes* in a place we recently visited or moved to for fear of kidnappings or being cheated by dubious and cunning fellows who took advantage of newcomers. I believed it was the same everywhere in the world. But the tone with which he spoke made me feel comfortable to some extent.

"I've been in your shoes before and I'm still there," he said. I nodded like I knew what he was talking about. "You'll soon figure out what's wrong, I assure you."

I was about to pull the handle of the restaurant door when he held my hands and smiled at me. I smiled back but deep within, I was judging his age. He looked young going by his smallish stature but looked like a man in his forties going by his beard.

"When you finally figure out what's wrong, brother," he began, "Don't feel bad. Just create your mantra and live by it. It'll help your confidence." He pulled the handle himself this time and walked through the door on to the road. A group of teenagers passed by us into the restaurant with bulgy eyes and dropping jaws. While I was busy trailing the kids with my eyes in a state of confusion, the bearded Indian said aloud, "Told you so, brother. We're in the same shoes."

The events during the first away match continued to replay in my memory. It still feels like a bad dream. I beckoned on my teammate, Jayden, to pass me the ball. He ignored my calls and gave me a look that spoke volumes. After five minutes, when my mesmerising movement meant I had a clear sight of goal, I called out to Ario, the German with twisted dreadlocks, to pass me the ball. To my dismay, he wore a blank look and mouthed, "Go to hell."

"How dare you say that to me?" I charged at him, overwhelmed with rage. Ario was unruffled. His words felt like a drill sunk into my bone marrow. I heard a chorus of boos from the crowd and the referee's whistle for full time made my boiling blood simmer. I wanted to show him the sinister side of me. He threw a triumphant smile at me, knowing I was battling with the fury within. I'm not sure but I believe I saw him poke his middle finger at me as we headed out of the field.

"This is not the end," I consoled myself.

The picture was starting to become clear to me. Each time I looked myself in the mirror, my reflection yelled the answer to the questioning stares and unfair treatment I received in the city and on the field. I never knew I was black until I arrived in Europe. The only thing I knew was that I was a few shades darker than the usual dark. My friends called me charcoal or baba dudu but only on few occasions and as a praise remark rather than a taunt. It never crossed my mind that racial debates will hang loosely like a mist over sound judgement. The bearded Indian was right. I cut out a cardboard sheet and wrote on it with a marker pen, I AM NOT INFERIOR. And on another, I wrote BLACK IS NOT A SYNONYM FOR INFERIOR, and hung them on my wall in my apartment. I had to come up with a mantra that could guide a newcomer like me until I was able to find my feet.

My best revenge was the way I thrilled the audience and viewers with the manner in which I dribbled and scored in almost every match. It was indeed, a sweet revenge to every pill of racism that was thrown at me. I bedazzled opponents with sheer wizardry, ghosting past at will and I became known in a short while as the footballing deity of Europe.

In buses, on trains, and even on the football field, it was a new experience altogether. Whenever I went shopping or sightseeing in town, eyes that spoke in a gasp of silence devoured me. There was a faint voice that constantly pricked at my conscience till I was enveloped in sweat always feeling like unwanted groceries left in the shopping cart because of my skin colour. Even the air I inhaled was unwelcoming. Sometimes, it had a foul stench.

At other times, it wore a shade of sorrow I found hard to comprehend.

I remembered the tales my uncle told me as a kid when he was studying for his degree in one of the European countries: how a ceiling of limitation was placed on him. I took my uncle's words with a pinch as he was renowned for exaggerating issues and adding 'pepper and other condiments' to spice up his stories. Biting his nails, my uncle would always start by telling us how he got a job with a Blue-chip Multinational Company shortly after his graduation but was stuck in one position for so many years. Incompetent colleagues who were undeserving always got promoted before him, which was painful to him and still leaves a gaping hole in his heart to date. That was the only wound difficult for time to heal, as his sour facial expression implied. He often told us the same tale before dinner in my family home: "As long as you are black, you are deemed as not good enough." He usually said this with deep pain clouding his face. I could tell that was one encounter in which the hurt would follow him to the grave.

"Ikemefuna, I want you to forget the wrangling on and off the pitch," Coach Boris Drinkfanta told me during a meeting in his office. Sarcasm etched thickly on his veins with a veiled reference to my on-field issues with Ario and Jayden during the last match.

I replied cheekily, "I know what I am here for." I had no problem with winning titles and battles. My only problem was the fact that, for no justifiable reason, they found a problem with my kind of black. Gyan, the only other black footballer on the team, was the one who usually made me feel welcome. We had so much in common, apart from being united by the colour of our skin. We were both mesmerizing footballers, born in December 1995 and we had to be in harmony to win the race war that kept raging like a fierce thunderstorm, even with the turn of the century.

Gyan had recounted his experience as a longstanding member of the team to me some weeks back. When we stayed back in the cafe near the dressing room, after everyone had left. He admonished, "Don't always expect to be abused by only the away supporters. There are days your team supporters might turn on you and even the dressing room might be against you. Race issues are treated with levity and ordinarily, the club does not expect you to raise any issues with the press about your experience as a person of colour or write about your frustrations on social media. You're meant to man up, bottle it in and take it all in the chin pretending as if it's the new cool, the normal." My face shone with a hint of regret as if questioning my decision to ply my trade in Europe.

"Has anyone spoken about it, been defiant, and halted a match in annoyance at this anomaly?" I queried.

"Not at all," Gyan replied.

"Then, I'm afraid I might be the jinx breaker, not minding whose ox is gored." There was an air of confidence and self-worth about me as I spoke.

Gyan wore a look that suggested to me it might be an effort in futility which I might live to regret. "The peace at the club is very fragile." He gently placed the mug on the table, careful to shift it to the middle where it balanced properly. For some weird reason, he felt the mug was a representation of the peace they were currently enjoying in the club, and he was scared that if he broke it, it would fast-track the disintegration of all they struggled to keep together. "I would advise you not to stoke discord in the dressing room as you do not want to fan the embers of the fury of the club's hierarchy, considering you're new here."

His endearing words did not make me reconsider my stance. He noticed my unconvinced countenance and added with a tone of finality, "A footballer's career is short lived, and you do not want to be mired in controversies that might end your European adventure before it even kicked off officially."

My first home match was against Bayern, the title holders. This was the best chance to announce my arrival to the whole of Europe and showcase my tremendous football skills where it mattered. As I walked on the football pitch with my shoulders held high, a chorus of boos echoed in and around the stadium. I waltzed through, deaf to their quest to wind me up. I saw a minority of home supporters join my abusers in what was an attempt to intimidate and bring me to submission. My team won the match by three goals to nil while I was named the man of the match after scoring one and assisting another goal. Shortly after, in the dressing room, the coach sent another player Mikael Fiona to speak to the press in my stead. The decision befuddled me, but I did my best to mask my disappointment. Gyan's admonition began to ring true. This had every colouration of subtle racism.

In the evening after the match, I met up with Gyan to have dinner and meet his wife for the first time.

"Meet my sunshine, Antonia," Gyan said with a smug. "Antonia meet the next African giant." This time he sounded outlandish. I exchanged pleasantries with Antonia. I noticed her skin glow in the Ankara prints that she wore and her gait was a perfect fit for her straight legs.

"You're a lucky fella," I said as soon as Antonia disappeared from view.

"I know, right."

Gyan had played no part in the football match as he was recovering from a metatarsal injury that had kept him on the side-lines seven months and counting.

"That was a great game to announce your arrival here," he cheered.

"Thanks man. Your presence here has made it easier for me to survive as a sheep amid rampaging bulls." My eyes met Antonia's as she returned to the lounge.

Gyan began his sermon, "You see, there are times you need to delay reaction. You need to think deeply about offensive conduct and give the appropriate response at the right time. Don't ever give a spur-of-the-moment reaction as you might lose your head and the outcome, distasteful."

His words hit home. Caution was the name of the game and I had to be at my very best to halt dissenting voices. Antonia waded into our conversation, "Be wary that everyone has a set of bias they are accustomed to and reacting negatively won't be the best outcome for everyone involved." After she was done admonishing me, she announced that the table was served. On the table was a sumptuous Ghanaian Chicken and Peanut Soup, which I devoured heartily. That reminded me of how much I miss home.

At night in my apartment, the Cable News channel was highlighting protests in the outskirts of the city where armed police officers had, through recklessness, killed innocent victims. The people of the community protested carrying placards with the inscription 'Black lives matter.' Deep down, I felt it was retrogressive and nauseating for us to be carrying banners with inscriptions 'Black lives matter' when inclusion and diversity should be our new swansong. "The labour of Martin Luther King Jr. and all the other black rights activists seems to be in futility," I pondered. "That is farther than the truth and our reality." I took a visit to the crime scene the next morning to empathise with the people and make enquiries. The undertone of fear and insecurity in the voices of the witnesses moved me. There was a white reporter gathering interviews from those who cared to speak as a follow-up to the previous report. I stared in her direction with angry eyes, expecting her to request an interview with me but when her eyes met mine, she turned away swiftly and began heading for the reporting booth.

"Excuse me," I called out to her. She stopped and turned, and I began walking up to her. "I have something to say. Put the camera on record."

She stared at me with nearly bulgy eyes as if afraid that I might be a suicide bomber. For a few seconds, she was silent. Only her eyes spoke.

"Okay," she said, awakening from her little slumber.

The microphone before me and the camera on my face, I began, "These are lives, people, whether black or white. Everyone is supposed to matter. I'm not expected to ignore a dying Caucasian or Mongoloid just because I don't have their complexion. If the police are protecting people, we should be included and not killed. Blacks are people too."

After the interview, I felt like an activist, proud that I had lent my voice to the course of humanity. I decided to use my newfound fame as a footballer of repute to advance the cause of my people and fight for their rights. There and then, I started to realise that footballing wasn't an end in itself for me but a means to achieve an end. I became an anchor for the black movement and printed over two hundred shirts with the inscription, BLACK LIVES MATTER in preparation for a peaceful protest I intended organising after the forthcoming championship games.

Back to the football pitch, I began training for the European Champions League final which was scheduled for Bulgaria. About one billion viewers were expected to tune in. My day of glory had finally arrived. From playing for Shoot for the Stars, a football club on the back side of Ibadan and mesmerizing opponents in continental football, I had the chance to showcase my exceptional talent to the entire world. My eyes still feel hazy and I wonder in amazement if my imagination was playing a fast one on me. Match day arrived with pomp and pageantry. In less than fifteen minutes, I had banged in a spectacular hat-trick on the biggest stage in World football.

As I celebrated my third goal I revealed a white tee shirt with the inscription, BLACK LIVES MATTER. The referee gave me a yellow card as a reprimand for my action. When the giant clock rested on thirty minutes, some football fans started to throw ripened bananas at me near the corner flag where I was to take a corner kick. Monkey chants drowned a section of the ***Stoichkov stand***. I unfurled one banana with shaky hands and the ball boy, Harry, unfurled two in solidarity. We sat down on the pitch and began eating. With the universe watching, the referee warned me to return to the pitch or else he would send me off. I ignored. The monkey chants were becoming pitch high like relentless rain. My eyes were burning red and my black skin gathered dust by the second. This was supposed to be my night of glory, turning to a charade of monumental proportions.

"Let's walk off this pitch," I screamed at my teammates. My words faded into thin air and didn't carry much weight as they all looked unfazed.

I turned around, ready to make a ***ridiculous move*** with the world watching. I thought of Gyan and his wife, how they would see me as a headstrong young man. I thought of my chances of being disqualified from the team. My heart began to pound for fear. But then, I thought of the numerous blacks like me who had gone through similar ordeals like what was happening right before me in the stadium. My heart stopped pounding in an instant. I summoned the courage, ready to make the ***ridiculous move***. The

European football federation president, sensing my body language, grabbed the microphone and brought the match to a disappointing close.

My three goals had won the Champions League for Borussia and I became a uniting factor together with Harry the ball boy for equality around the world. As I lifted the Champions League trophy with the World watching, the over two hundred tee shirts with the inscription BLACK LIVES MATTER that I printed had been shared in a section around the stadium and it was a stunning spectacle to behold. I cried tears of joy hearing the people chant my name all around the stadium till the water in my eyes was no more.

IN THE TRAP OF SEERS

The stridulating sounds of the night's crickets were loud in Iyanu's ears as she separated her eyelids from one another to see Mami's face right before hers. Mami's lips were moving and her eyes shone wide. At first, Iyanu presumed Mami was devouring the fufu and ewedu soup she had spent hours diligently preparing. She jumped up in shock that she would end up not having to taste the sumptuous meal, ever. But a few seconds after, reality dawned on her.

"Iyanu! I said wake up!" Mami commanded in a loud whisper. "Get dressed. We're going to see Baba Akinwande at Akinyele."

Iyanu had almost forgotten their appointment with the babalawo. Her eyes were heavy with sleep but she managed to pull her long, thin self off the bed and into the bathroom. Mami was already dressed in an Adire blouse and wrapper. Iyanu would have guessed her outfit right without looking at her. Her wardrobe housed more Adires than Aso oke, Laces and Ankaras.

"Sew them big," she would tell the tailor. She preferred to wear oversized clothes in order to look robust like the other women in the neighbourhood in Oluyole. If she didn't do so, they would ask, "Mama Iyanu, any problem? You're emaciating o…" It was embarrassing that nearly everyone knew her challenges- a broken marriage and a daughter whom in her heart she called a miscreant. Her way out of the numerous sympathetic questions was to wear bogus clothes even though her thin legs, when she wore shorter wrappers and skirts, betrayed her efforts.

"Mami, let's go," Iyanu tapped her mother, who had fallen asleep on the couch of their small living room while waiting for her. She got up swiftly as if she were as light as paper, slung her famous bag across her shoulders and re-tied her wrappers before exiting the door. There was a sac by the door she picked up gently in which *kee-kee-run* sounds proceeded while she headed out. As they walked by their neighbour's gate, she hushed Iyanu, whose feet were scraping against the tarred road.

"It's only 1am. Nobody in Oluyole must know we're out by this time."

"Okay, Mami," Iyanu replied. She clutched her body with both arms jittering from the cold water she had poured on her skin in the bathroom. She hated bathing in cold water during the Harmattan season, but Mami had banned her from boiling water in a kettle with the gas cylinder.

"Gas is expensive and you contribute no income to this house. All you do is waste my resources," she would say.

The walk to Baba Akinwande's shrine was as annoying as his short height to Iyanu. She had to pass through thickets and bushes, sweep the dust with her feet and climb over rocky stones to get there. Oluyole, where they lived, was now a distance behind them and Akinyele was still some distance ahead. If not for the power he had boasted to have, she would have been defiant to walking such a long and bumpy distance. It was Mrs. Lukman, the neighbour whose mannerisms reflected her name, who introduced Mami to Baba Akinwande. She had dramatically narrated how he exposed all the witches behind her barrenness and asked her to move on to another husband. "My sister, that was how he cured my barrenness o." She dragged the 'o' and rounded off with a clap. Mami was moved by the story but Iyanu wasn't. She calculated that Mrs. Lukman wasn't barren in the first place if she had a child in her second marriage. After all, her first husband was now remarried and yet to have a child with his new wife, so, how did Baba Akinwande cure her barrenness? It was common sense he applied.

Mami secured an appointment with Baba Akinwande through Mrs. Lukman immediately after the conversation and by the next night, they were on their way there for their first visit. Iyanu had imagined a standard apartment as his consultation room due to the various powerful testimonies Mrs. Lukman ascribed to him but to her dismay, it was a ramshackle environment filled with calabashes of spirogyra water, weeds, dirty pieces of clothes and what looked like skeleton skulls that she believed she could craft with clay herself. She chuckled when Mami yelped at one that stared her right in the face as she drew open the curtains of the hot and smelly consultation room made of thatched materials.

Standing before them was Baba Akinwande, who told them to bring two *tolotolo* along with them for spiritual cleansing during the next visit. He said that the blood of the animals would be used to wash Iyanu's feet, hands and head. There was barely any money in Mami's purse but she readily agreed to Baba Akinwande's demands as long as it was going to change Iyanu's life. Now, as they walked through the bush, Mami held tightly the sac in her hand as if it were gold, hoping that at the death of the turkeys and the sprinkling of their blood, her daughter's destiny would come alive. She would be the somebody expected of her.

"I know you're tired but we're almost there," Mami consoled as they walked through the bush.

"Yes, ma."

"You know, powerful men like this have to be in hiding where they can access the gods."

"Yes, ma."

"I assure you, by the time he's done with you, you will be the next Oprah Winfrey."

"Yes, Ma."

"Iyanu, say something other than yes ma."

"Yes, Ma."

There was nothing else Iyanu could say. She doubted strongly that Baba Akinwande could cast away the demons she had come to believe by Mami's conviction were attacking her destiny. They had paid visits to five seers already and nothing had changed. After their visits to the last two, she had vowed not to deprive herself of what she called her delicious sleep for night journeys to any seer whatsoever.

Alufa Ijo was the previous one before the last. He was the exact opposite of Baba Akinwande. Tall, thin, Albino whereas Baba Akinwande was short, fat and black like charcoal. Iyanu likened him to a Guinness bottle. Not that his shade of dark was a problem but she had a disgust for him she couldn't explain.

Alufa Ijo's shrine was organized compared to Akinwande's but wasn't impressive either. He had a bench by the wall for visitors on which they sat when they arrived. There was a standing fan beside them that *biggled* and *baggled* as it rotated, blowing air that smelled like burning electric wire. Iyanu had remarked that they might die of unhealthy air in the waiting room but Mami hushed her immediately, saying, "Don't insult the holy ground."

When Alufa Ijo's servant ushered them into the consultation room, the first thing Iyanu noticed was Alufa Ijo staring right at her chest. There were two sofas opposite each other, red curtains shielding the windows and nothing else. The room was almost empty. Alufa requested that Iyanu sit directly opposite him while Mami sat next to her. She was sure he wanted to have a good look at her well rounded breasts.

"What's your challenge?"

"Holy One, it's my daughter not me. She's not a good head. Nothing works for her and she keeps getting into trouble. All her mates are either in the university or have graduated. Some are even married with a child or two but her case is always on the negative."

"How old is she?"

"Twenty-three, Holy One."

He sniffed and spat as if he could smell the presence of a demon. He began mentioning the name, BJ. Mami leaned forward with keen interest.

"Holy One, we have a relative called Uncle BJ. Could he be the demon?"

Iyanu threw a glance at the 'holy one.' He threw her a glance too but his eyes went down her face to her neck and then settled on her chest. She felt a movement in her left breast as if it was aware of his eyes. He stretched his hand to a calabash beside him and lifted it in the air, saying things neither women could understand. While he did that, Iyanu was busy scrutinising him from head to toe. She noticed something and stopped at it. His manhood hidden behind the red wrapper he wore was up like the head of a snake ready to bite. There was a surge of anger in her as she looked from him to Mami whose eyes were focused on the hanging calabash between Alufa Ijo's palms.

"She needs to be examined in the spirit room," Alufa cut in through the silence.

"Or you need to examine me with your needle?"

"Iyanu!" Mami exclaimed. "Don't you ever talk to the holy one like that again."

The visit was a futile one as the women strode back home in silence. Iyanu had opted out of the spiritual cleansing exercise without apology. She hoped that her mother would not bring up another talk of another seer but she was wrong. Barely a week after their angry return from Alufa Ijo's place, Mami brought up the talk of Babaleye, a prominent seer whose miracles in the city were widely documented. Iyanu had heard so much about him, that he had so many hidden secrets that would pierce hearts once revealed. At first, she declined, but a look at Mami's clavicles which were overly visible as a result of stress, worry and depression changed her mind. Anything that would make her mother happy became her priority even though it was against her wish. She threw a glance at the big, brown envelope that laid untouched on the dining table and let out a big sigh.

* * * * *

The letter of notice of expulsion laid on the table in its envelope. Iyanu's parents sat still and quiet on the sofa while she stood before them, waiting for some tongue lashing as usual. She wasn't sorry when she was caught in bed with Ibrahim, the neighbour's son; she wasn't sorry when her H.O.D called her father to inform him that she was advised to repeat two hundred level; she wasn't sorry for her numerous atrocities, including smoking Ijebu weed. But this time, the expulsion letter, after a fight with one of her course mates over a boy they liked, humbled her. Mami cast her gaze to the floor in a bid to allow the tears in her eyes drop. Papa Iyanu fixed his gaze on the kitchen doorway as if expecting a cook to walk through bearing a tray of food. Iyanu wanted to break the silence; she wanted to say she was sorry for breaking their hearts for being a nasty nineteen-year-old but she didn't. Her choice of study was Fine and Applied Arts but they chose Law. She enjoyed painting artworks on cardboard and wooden boards, and sometimes, crafted gourds and figurines with clay. Painting and sculpting were her forte but Papa Iyanu said he wanted his daughter to live a legacy he could not fulfill so he insisted she studied Law. The dates and jargon and numerous quotes that proceeded from the mouths of the lecturers made Iyanu know, right from the first lecture that she would never make a good lawyer.

The silence was piercing, irritating. Neither of them had opened the envelope. They avoided it like it was a letter bomb. They only knew the content of the envelope because Iyanu had let them in on it.

"I know I'm stupid but please say something," Iyanu pleaded, breaking the long silence.

Just curse me. Hit me. Throw me out. Anything.

She wanted them to ease the tension in the atmosphere with whatever they had in mind. She wanted to know her fate. But rather than say anything, Papa Iyanu got up from the sofa and grabbed his car keys from the centre table. His height equalled hers. He looked sideways at her from up to down for some seconds and turned towards the door.

"Where are you going to?" Mami finally spoke up, her face searching his as if trying to read his unspoken words.

"Away from this bastard child!" He yelled. It was deafening, not because it was loud but because the word 'bastard' stung the atmosphere.

"Ah! You are calling your own blood a bastard!"

"She's not my blood. I don't have bad blood running through my veins. It's either she's fighting and getting in trouble, expecting us to bail her with money, or she's failing her exams woefully, or she's having indiscriminate sex with the neighbourhood boys. And now, this. I can't stand it anymore."

"Papa Iyanu…"

"Don't call me that anymore. I cease to be her father, henceforth. Rather than bear me a son, you bore me a tout for a daughter. I'm going in search of a son, myself."

"Ah…! mo gbe! e gba mi! You are leaving me too!"

Papa Iyanu didn't answer. He walked straight to the door and slammed it behind him, leaving Mami jumping up and down in tears, making promises to try harder in giving him a son even though they all knew she was way past her menopause. She threw herself to the floor and rolled from one end to another while Iyanu watched in pity, not for her mother but for herself. From childhood, she had heard her father yell at her mother several times to give him a son. At first, she prayed that Mami's womb would open up for a boy so she could have a brother, but the day her father hit her mercilessly for a mere mistake she had made in her Mathematics assignment, saying, "I wouldn't have even cared about you if I had a son," she changed her prayer point to *God, I don't need a brother anymore. Don't allow Mami to get pregnant again.* Once, Mami scolded her in Yoruba when she failed to do her morning duties, "You are a useless child, and until I have another one, I will never feel like a parent." Although, she apologised days later with words and gifts and extra fish in her dishes, those words haunted Iyanu for a good part of her life.

Iyanu looked through the window watching her father drive out of the compound in his Lexus away from Oluyole, Ibadan to a faraway place she would later come to know was Yaoundé, Cameroon. And she would earnestly pray for his return from that day not because she wanted to see him but because she wanted Mami to smile again. Her lips quivered, her heartbeat increased its pace, her eyes blinked and her hands trembled as she walked into the inner chambers of the house knowing she was the reason her parents had just split. She prayed to God in her heart to make her a boy, should she have a second life. That night, she dreamt of seers dancing and clapping around her, diagnosing her problems.

* * * * *

"Pour Omo inside the water very well," someone shouted. Mami and Iyanu heard the voice from afar and halted. For a moment, they thought of running into hiding for fear of robbers and cultists, but the rise of smoke in the atmosphere made them curious enough to draw closer. Baba Akinwande was in view, running helter skelter with his servants, buckets in hands, throwing water here and there at the flames that engulfed his shrine. Mami's eyes widened at the chaotic sight. She dumped the sac in her hand and ran forward to join in the rescue.

"The gods have been burned! The gods have been burned!" Baba Akinwande kept screaming as one of his servants emptied a full five kilograms Omo sachet into his bucket. Iyanu watched from a corner with narrow eyes and lips curved in a downward arc. Although, she neither liked him nor believed in him, she secretly hoped that his spiritual cleansing exercise would eliminate her demons for the sake of her mother's happiness and peace.

When the fire was finally put out, the entire shrine was burned. Baba Akinwande sat on the sandy ground sorrowfully while his servants looked on at the sorry sight. Mami stood by them feeling their pain.

"Holy One, can the spiritual cleansing still take place?" she asked with trembling voice. There was no response. Iyanu wanted to tell her the gods had been burned and he has lost his power, but she cautioned herself. She rather placed a palm on her shoulders and whispered, "Mami, let's go."

The next morning, Iyanu pulled the turkeys out of the sac, untied them and let them stray away from the compound to wherever they listed. She had watched a Nollywood film, sometime ago, of how a seer had placed his upper and lower teeth on the neck of a fowl and bit off its head. She was sure Baba Akinwande was going to do the same to the poor animals; maybe this time, twist their necks in circular motion until they were out of breath and their heads were pulled off. *Better that his dirty, ugly shrine burned down than for the animals to die ruthlessly.* Mami had borrowed from Mrs. Lukman to buy them but she didn't care. All she wanted was to see them live; after all, the seers only cared about their pockets and pots, demanding either money or cooking items. Babaleye, the last seer they visited after Alufa Ijo, had collected the sum of one hundred thousand naira to conduct a sacrifice to ward away the demons that subdued her destiny, with the assurance that something great would happen in her life before the year ran out. When nothing was forthcoming, he gave the excuse that her case was too complicated.

Once the animals were out of sight, Iyanu walked to the backyard where her sculpting materials and tools lay. She bent towards them and began measuring clay for a dancing girl she intended sculpting. Tears began pouring from her eyes, and rather than mould with water, she moulded with her tears. Until she was done with the process, her tears flowed ceaselessly. She was beginning to wonder if she really had demons that didn't want her to be a 'good head.' The way her mother wept on their return from Akinyele made her wonder what was wrong with her, why her life was stagnant. Could it be that her demons were fighting the seers in order to keep her tied down?

"What have you moulded?" Mami asked from behind as Iyanu picked the figure from the platform where she had put it to dry. It was dusk already.

"I wanted to mould a dancing girl but I ended up moulding this." She handed the sculpted face to her mother. Mami rubbed it from top to bottom, smiling at it.

"Thank you." It was her. Iyanu sculpted her face. "It's beautiful."

"You're beautiful, Mami. I know I've failed you and I'm determined to work hard to make things right."

Mami was silent. She cast her gaze to the cattle egrets that flew across the sky in an orderly manner, observing how bright and beautiful they were. "There's this imam I would like you to meet," she began, lowering her eyes back to Iyanu. "They say he has performed a number of miracles. He might have the solution to your problem."

Iyanu rolled her eyes and pouted her lips as she listened. There was no iota of surprise on her face. After yesterday's event, she didn't expect her mother to give up on seers. Her only surprise was the shift from traditionalists to a religious leader.

"I would go wherever you ask me to if it makes you happy," Iyanu replied. It pleased Mami's heart and she smiled again, this time at her. For a moment, she felt sorry for all the times she thought her to be a miscreant. Now, all she wanted was to see a girl who lived the meaning of her name: Miracle.

The following weeks were filled with visits to imams and prophets who diagnosed her problems. Names of extended family members were mentioned as being responsible for her *slow motion movement* in life. Two Imams said Uncle JJ had swapped her star for his, and two prophets said Uncle TJ had stolen her destiny through gifts he bought for her as a kid. One placed them on a forty-day fast for the death of Uncle JJ and another placed them on a thirty-day vigil so Uncle TJ could confess. On days when Iyanu was weary from the fast, Mami said, "Omo Ologo ni e," reminding her of Jesus. Iyanu often pondered where her mother belonged. Today, she prayed in the name of Jehovah. Another day, she prayed in the name of the supreme being of Islam. Sometimes, in the name of the gods of the various traditional seers they had visited. She often remarked, "Iyanu, the demons in your father's house swapped your ever-shining glory for a dimly lit one; hence, your adversity. So, we have to pray in the name of as much supreme beings as possible."

* * * * *

The house was empty. Every pot clang and door creak sounded louder than usual, echoing through the house like it were a tunnel. The lights were off and the curtains were down, making the living room look like dusk at noon. Iyanu was by the window scooping rice in tiny quantities from a ceramic bowl she held in her hand, which sounded *ting ting* at every scoop. The window reminded her of the moment her father walked out on them in his Lexus. She smiled at the memory of the Lexus. The day Papa Iyanu first drove it into the compound, Mami had run out in jubilation. It was a clean, gold car, what the neighbours called 'tear rubber.' Mami hurried into the driver's seat as soon as Papa Iyanu stepped out, and began turning the steering from side to side as if cruising the car, saying, "Voom! Voom! Voom!" Papa Iyanu laughed hard as he watched his semi-literate wife celebrate the brand new car like a kid pulling at her gift by a Christmas tree. "It will be yours if you give me a son this year," he said as he bent towards her, his head in the car, his body out, and kissed her lips passionately while five-year old Iyanu watched innocently. That was the first and only time she saw her parents kiss; other times, Papa Iyanu was either giving Mami orders or yelling at her over his need for a son.

At first, it was the emptiness of the spot where the Lexus was parked that made her lose her appetite, but now, it was the emptiness of the house since Mami died last week. She blamed herself for Mami's death. She blamed herself for her inability to put a smile on her face before departing. She blamed herself for so many things. Since Mami's death, her tongue had not tasted anything besides water until now when she just had to fill her rumbling belly. She knew Mami loved her dearly except that she lacked the right ways to express her love. She had also come to understand that the times Mami treated her wrongly were times she was under pressure to bear a son.

The spoon slipped from Iyanu's right hand as she heard a knock on the door. First, she thought she heard the sound from within the house and imagined Mami's ghost must be around, but another knock confirmed it was from without. She opened the door to see Mrs. Lukman with a black dress in her hand which she had promised to sew for her through the tailor in the neighbourhood.

"Your father called. He called to say he would be coming over for the burial next week," Mrs. Lukman said, handing over the poorly sewn black dress to Iyanu while peering into the living room from where she stood. There was always something to look at or stare at and Iyanu was not surprised. Mrs. Lukman was also in a black dress. Since Mami's death, every outfit she wore was either black, white, or had a touch of black and white. Iyanu always doubted the sincerity of her friendship with Mami but the colour of her clothes and the way she stopped by to check on her every now and then, made her believe that whatever she felt for Mami was genuine.

"Okay, Ma," Iyanu replied soberly, only glancing at the dress. On a normal day, she would have scrutinised it and complained bitterly. But now, there was no energy for such. Just before she said goodbye to Mrs. Lukman, even though, she knew she would come again in the evening to say *sorry* and *ndo* and *it is well*, the woman consoled once more.

"Iyanu, *pele*. Sorry ehn… All will be well with time. You'll get over your mother's death soon."

She wished it was that easy. Every night, she saw Mami in her dreams stretching out her hand, calling to her for help. She would see herself running towards her to pull her by the hand but before she is able to, her mother would disappear, and she would wake up screaming and crying. Sleep would be gone from her eyes and she would spend the remaining hours of the night pacing up and down the house, recalling how it all happened.

* * * * *

Days of hunger and nights of sleeplessness, yet, nothing seemed to happen. The imams and prophets urged that the women exercise faith and patience until their miracles arrived. At first, they obeyed but news of Uncle BJ's promotion in the oil firm he worked in Lagos, news of Uncle JJ throwing a party for the delivery of his fourth child and first son in the UK, and news of Uncle TJ, who lived in Uyo, buying a brand new Toyota Venza threw them into depression.

"The opposite of faith is depression," one of the prophets admonished earlier, "and depression is lack of trust in Jah. The moment you fall into depression, you lose your miracle. Unless you pay a sum of one hundred and fifty thousand naira so my prayer warriors and I can intercede on your behalf."

Going by the prophet's words, they concluded they had lost their miracle and since they had no money to pay for intercession, they ended their fast on the thirtieth day. Iyana thought that the end of visits to seers had come and she would have danced for joy but for the day- four days after they ended their fast- Mami came again with tales of one Alfa Seriki who was nicknamed 'Oracle of the Supreme.'

"But Mami, we have no more money to buy goats and turkeys and snails, neither do we have to dash these men."

"I know my child, but it is foolishness to throw to the cocks what is valuable." This, Mami said in

Yoruba. Then, she continued in English, "Finding a solution to your problem and taking it for granted is foolhardy."

"Fine. I'll go. But promise me that we'll visit no more seer after this."

"I promise. This is our last."

Alfa Seriki was of average height and slim. His low-cut hair was curly and a lighter shade of black but Iyanu thought it was dirty; hence, the colour. When he opened his mouth to speak, Iyanu would first look away before adjusting her gaze back to his face. The stench he produced was horrible and gave the answer to the question why his teeth were brownish black. As usual, he spoke about demons and principalities and powers under the heavens but rather than focus on his revelations, Iyanu kept herself busy pondering his ethnicity by his looks. *I think he's a Nok. Abi no. His curly hair gives me the impression he's a Fulani. Just that his fluent Yoruba and his name makes it look like he's one of us.* The sound of "*Odo-ona*" jolted her from her thoughts.

"We're going to do what?" She asked.

"I said you two will need a spiritual bath in *Odo-ona Elewe River*," Alfa said, throwing his tongue around his dark, flaky lips.

"That's too deep a river for people like us who can't swim, Alfa. What about the streams here in Eleyele?"

"I won't wash you in the deep. Just a little bit farther from the shore."

Iyanu refused vehemently but Mami's consistent patting on her lap from beneath the table that separated them from Alfa Seriki weakened her. She wanted to say more but she lost the strength to. Mami was not the type of person she could make to see things from her viewpoint.

"Holy One, we'll come with you to *Odo-Ona*," Mami cut in to ease the atmosphere.

"12a.m tomorrow."

The trip to *Odo-ona* was as hectic as the walk to Baba Akinwande's shrine except that there were no thickets and thorns to pull apart, just sandy ground on which they marched barefooted and clad in white garments. They had initially presumed Alfa would drive them in his *kabu kabu* Mazda but he told them to walk it with him as a sign of readiness for the spiritual exercise. Mami considered it the end of all traumas and problems while Iyanu hoped it wouldn't end in chaos the way it ended for them at Baba Akinwande's. Above them, a colony of bats flew across filling the atmosphere with their clicks and pings. Iyanu bent over for a dodge even though they were far up in the sky. Her skin developed goosebumps suddenly and she drew near to her mother whispering her fears. She hated bats and whenever she saw them, she smelled a bad omen. Sometimes, she was right. Sometimes, she was wrong.

"Stay calm. All is well," Mami assured.

Odo-ona was right before them, splashing here and there with the wave tides. Alfa walked ahead of them into the water and stopped. Soon, they joined him.

"This place is just deep enough for the spirits to commune with us," he said and began whistling. It was his way of telling the spirits he had arrived. After a minute, he stopped and turned to the women.

"Who's going first?"

"Definitely not me," Iyanu retorted. Mami was pissed off. *This stubborn child of mine* was the phrase that swept through her mind but she refrained from scolding her in the presence of Alfa. With a raise of her right hand, she signalled herself as being ready. He took her hand in his and led her few steps further which bothered Iyanu. They had gone waist deep in the water. Alfa placed his hand on her head and lowered her into the water while still holding her other hand. One dip. Two dips. Three dips. And that was it. Iyanu took in a deep breath from where she stood, happy that there was no casualty. But as Mami tried to make her way out of the rising ocean, she lost her footing and slipped into the water. Alfa lost her hand as he tried to grab her. Iyanu screamed and ran further into the water but Alfa ran after her and pulled her out with him. She attempted fighting his hands off her waistline but he was too strong for her to contend with.

"Allow me save my mother!" she screamed.

"You don't want to die, do you?" His response amazed her. She looked into his eyes, moving her eyeballs from one end to another as if searching for an iota of humanity in him.

"You led my mother into the deep and you left her there to drown, yet, you ask if I want to die?" Her heart bled as she spoke. She looked on at the water pondering what next step to take. Swimming wasn't something she was good at.

"Alfa, do something!"

"I can't. The waves are too much for me to handle. I'm sorry."

At that moment, Iyanu fell to her knees and let out a loud cry. Her heart began to pound and her lips began to quiver more than they did when her father drove out of the compound and away from them. She tried to lift her hands but they trembled so greatly that they dropped back by her sides. Alfa placed his hand at her back to console her but she fought him off. The demons were winning, and she was losing this battle badly.

It wasn't until three weeks later that Mami's badly mutilated body was found by the seashore by the Rescue Squad of the police.

* * * * *

The weight of Mami's death bore heavily on Iyanu as Mami's cold and pale body lay in the casket. The compound was filled with family members and well-wishers, among whom were Uncle TJ, Uncle BJ and Uncle JJ and their wives. They had brought wreaths along with them to pay respect to Mami. Iyanu sighted them under the canopy and made efforts to avoid their gaze. But for her father, she looked around to no avail. She was in her poorly sewn black dress seated by Mrs. Lukman who spent the whole time crying, "oluwa o! oluwa o!" as family members and friends read out good words and phrases that described the deceased. Soon, it was her turn. She put up a display as she took a stand by the casket, almost falling into it. Those seated in front hurried to her and held her till she dramatically steadied herself on her feet.

"Hey! Hey! Hey!" she began, "Mama Iyanu, hey!" The interjection, hey, constituted the majority of the words in her speech, and she went on and on without keeping to the five minutes allotted to her until the pastor in charge cut short her speech. She walked back to her seat clutching her chest like one who was shivering from cold. Iyanu would have laughed but the event was too hollow for her to stretch the edge of her lips an inch.

As the casket was being laid six feet below, it suddenly dawned on Iyanu that her mother was truly gone. Somehow, she secretly hoped and imagined that her mother would appear from somewhere alive and hale. But now, she knew all those were hallucinations. The heaviness in her heart grew worse that she had to walk through the midst of the people quietly into the house where she could cry out until she was satisfied. From the doorway of the living room, Iyanu sighted someone who looked familiar. He was standing by the dining table staring at a paper in his hand.

"Papa?" She was inside now, the door shut behind her.

Papa Iyanu looked sideways to where she stood and replied, "Iyanu." Then, he added, "My child," in a softer tone.

Iyanu couldn't believe her ears. Her run-away father who disowned her had acknowledged her as his child. She was caught up in a dilemma- to cry or to laugh. It was good news but at the same time, she was pissed that he did so only after Mami was gone. Her eyes strolled from his face to the paper in his hands. It was the letter of expulsion he and Mami had refused to open since she brought it home four years ago. There was a gush of wind that swept through the window of the dining room and blew the brown envelope from the table down to her feet. She bent over and picked it up.

"I failed you, Papa," she said, straightening herself on her feet again.

"No, you didn't. I did. I failed you and your mother." Mami's picture on the wall made a *knock knock* as if saying, "You sure did." The wind was getting stronger, blowing everything in the house- the curtains, the wooden frames on the wall, the upholstered chairs. "I always wanted to study law but never did. My father could only afford me a college of education degree with which I worked as a teacher before venturing into other businesses. So, I vowed that my son would be the lawyer that I couldn't be."

"And when you didn't have a son?" Iyanu asked, searching her father's eyes, which were now misty.

"I hated you," he replied. "I tried to love you but my anger at not having a son subdued my efforts to love you." Iyanu looked away from him but he rushed to her and grabbed her face in his palms pleadingly. "I couldn't even have another child in my second marriage, Iyanu. You're the only one that has my blood running through your veins." It wasn't news to Iyanu that her father had remarried a Cameroonian woman. Mrs. Lukman had gossiped it to Mami but how she found out, no one could tell.

There was a knock. Uncle JJ pushed the door open before Iyanu could permit. He was Mami's half-brother but they were never in good terms so they barely saw eyeball to eyeball. But now that she was dead, he decided to pay his last respect.

"How are you doing Iyanu?" he asked with a smile and a forged British accent.

"I'm fine, sir. And your baby?" Iyanu noticed he was now fair. The last time she saw him before he relocated to the UK, he was dark in complexion. *Men bleach too now*, she concluded in her heart.

"Baby is well, thanks." He shook his hand hurriedly in one of his pockets and pulled out a paper. It was a cheque of three million naira, which he handed over to her, telling her it was for her education. Iyanu's mouth went agape. She looked up at him from the cheque and back to it again. Papa Iyanu was standing behind her, amazed as well. Uncle JJ started to walk away, rubbing both hands against his trousers nervously but then, he stopped at the door and said before leaving, "I know your mother and I were never in good terms because our father stopped her education for mine, but this is the least I can do for her." He shut the door behind him, leaving Iyanu in her overwhelmed and speechless state.

In the days that followed, other gifts, monetary and material, flooded in. Some were from names she last heard when she was a kid or young teen, some from names she barely knew, and the others from familiar names. Many believed she was now orphaned and needed help, especially since she did nothing tangible to earn money. But the most shocking gift she would receive would be the call from her father after his return to Cameroon, to sponsor her education.

"Feel free to study Fine and Applied Arts, your chosen discipline," he would tell her.

* * * * *

A full length smiling sculpture of Mami stood upright in IYANIWURA ARTS GALLERY, Iyanu's sculpture garden, watching over the activities of people strolling in and out for sight-seeing and to buy the various objects on display.

"These are so lovely," one woman said to her husband as they stopped to admire three perfectly moulded horsemen. Iyanu was a few distances behind them in a brown coat, fringe hair extension, a pair of jeans and sneakers looking around in admiration. When her eyes met the sculpture of Mami, she paused and smiled in return. *It's been eight years, Mami and I miss you*, she lipped and pouted a kiss. Then, she laughed, recalling when Papa Iyanu revealed to her that Mami did not read the letter in the envelope on the dining table because she was poor at reading- something she had never known about her mother until then.

"Miss Iyanu," someone called. She looked behind to see Adekemi, her former intern and newest recruit at Iyaniwura Arts Gallery.

"A client called from Lagos requesting to buy one of the figurines for twenty thousand dollars," Adekemi informed.

"What? That's huge for the figurine. What did he say his name was?"

"Mr. Bolaji Johnson."

EVERYBODY DON KOLOMENTAL

BAGGAGE OF PROBLEMS

Everyone is kolomental in Lagos city. The panic that clouds the city during the rush hour traffic, and the street vendors who eke a living under the flaming afternoon sun among others, are tell-tale signs that mental health should be at the front burner. The yellow bus I entered on my way to school was rickety and looked like it would disintegrate fast. The bus conductor whom I later knew as Muftau looked angry, hungry, and malnourished. To survive life at the bus park, being tough and streetwise is a non-negotiable attribute. Muftau ticked all the right boxes. It's a race for the survival of the fittest. He looked scruffy and had a foul body odour that made the bus smell of decomposing food on a dunghill.

Muftau yelled at his passengers who were crammed into the bus. "Ti o ba ni change, you better get down from the bus now. Get down now o, because I no get change," he yelled repeatedly. Beside me was a woman, half asleep, breathing heavily and snoring in-between. Familiar stories of the rush hour train on London's underground swept through my core. I have never stepped foot outside the shores of Nigeria, but I have watched with keen interest on satellite television, a documentary detailing how busy the Jubilee line can be during peak period in London. I snapped back at him, "You should have said so before we entered this bus that looks like it's on a journey to hell." I saw the venom dance across his bulging eyeballs, threatening to dangle out of their sockets. It made me feel like I had awoken a sleeping lion.

The last person anyone should want to fight with is someone who has nothing to lose. Father would always say, "Those are worse than pigs because they don't mind losing their lives when engaged in a fight for any cause they believed in." Bus Conductors in Lagos city sit atop that list. The only other worthy contender for top honours would be the street urchins scattered around the city, trying every illegal method possible to eke out a living. As Muftau was about spitting fire, I brought out my headphones so I could begin listening to some good soul music from my new playlist titled '***Food for the Soul.***' It was a herculean task making those song selections, but days like this make it truly a worthwhile venture. Muftau could see the silent plea in my eyes. It was fuel scarcity season, and buses were increasingly hard to find, however rickety they were. I was ecstatic when the bus halted at the last bus-stop near the University gate and I alighted without giving any attention to Muftau. I could hear him murmuring, but the blaring music drowned his voice and I was delighted to get away without getting involved in a brawl.

The journey back home made me a nervous wreck. I still wonder why father bought a house near a worship centre. That means I was stuck here for some time to come, at least until I'm able to fend for myself or father becomes rich enough to buy another house. I don't know which is likely to happen first but with the current, it remains a pipe-dream. And I am a fantasist.

The blaring noise from the loudspeakers for the morning call to prayer was my alarm clock, my call to action. To make the best use of my day while others slumber through the dawn of morning till it slips away from their grasp. I had a deep-seated repugnance for it. I love a good night's sleep in solitude, one of the most important things in my life which the alarm denied me.

I dreaded home; the noise made me want to be away. Not with the constant migraine that strikes intermittently like a power outage in my city. I found comfort in unaccustomed terrains if there were no worship centres within proximity. Every time I came within close propinquity of a worship centre at night or before daylight, I would suffer panic attacks. I became a captive of my emotions and fear. That was my baggage of problems, a cross I had to carry. More like a cup of tea with no sweeteners. I could only be aggrieved but could not voice out my concerns else I became a martyr. I would rather leave that sacrosanct issue to another, as I love life to the fullest.

Everyone has a baggage of problems that needs a quick fix. Shindara, our next-door neighbour, has more than baggage. His was a truckload of problems; he kills demons, strange enemies, even familiar ones. His praying pattern is very melancholy. He shouts, screams and at other times weeps with a croaky voice. The Monday morning after Christmas celebrations, I met Shindara by the gate and asked him an innocent question. "Shindara, I know the world is teeming with many depraved people, but why not get busy?" The look on Shindara's face was lukewarm. I could tell he couldn't wait for me to round up this conversation as there were more enemies awaiting his holy assault.

I sounded like a broken record and the sound of my voice was irritating me. But I was undeterred.

You would think there was a prize award for me to tell it as it is. I felt I had an obligation to deliver Shindara from his mental slavery. I continued unapologetically, "All these demons you're killing, have they not finished? When will you finish killing them so you can get some work done on a Monday morning? You know the demons might not be the problem." I looked up only to discover that I had been talking into thin air. For how long, I couldn't tell. Shindara was nowhere to be found and that innocent conversation was the catalyst to the big wedge drawn between once upon a time, jolly neighbours. I consoled myself that I was excited my mouth is a home for truths, even though that's the easiest way to lose friends. I have lost count the number of friends I have lost in less than three months.

I know about demons and familiar enemies. I attended the fast-rising church on Fifth Avenue on the first Sunday of the new year, with a list of my New Year resolutions tightly squeezed into my palm. The white paper was beginning to get soaked from my sweaty palms as I patiently waited for us to pray our way into the New Year. Attending church on this day has been a ritual I have religiously obeyed over the last five years. The only time I chose to drink my way into the New Year. The year ended on a torrid note. The senior pastor made an altar call for those suffering from mental illness and before I could say wassup, there were a few hundred running to the altar as if the first person to get to the altar was the only person who would be made whole again.

I stole a swift glance to see if the ill-tempered spouse of the pastor would heed the '*altar call*' as she had almost tore the pastor's clothes to shreds during Christmas day service. She accused the pastor of going beyond the remit of his spiritual calling by having extra-marital affairs with some choristers in the sophisticated choir unit. The tension that day was palpable; there were flying chairs and broken legs. Some new converts were crestfallen and some devoted church members were ready to break an arm to protect God's anointed. They all came to one damning conclusion, '*the devil has built a hut in the heart of the Pastor's wife*' and she executed his schemes to the letter. In the weeks that followed, the allegations were swept under the carpet and the Pastor and his wife forged a chemistry, the kind so unseen that muted all dissenting voices that would have raised dust on the confusion in the holy chamber. A lot of workers in the vineyard tried to unearth what transpired between the pastor and his wife that made her heed the voice of reason. It remained a mystery no one could unravel.

Back to the current, I saw a multitude of heads and I spoke in what I thought were inaudible notes. "Too many mad people ***fill this city***. Madness knows no form and has no mother tongue, they also wear suits and drive big cars. The sad reality dawned on me that we all need help, and not everyone can afford therapy."

I had my personal demons to confront. They came in different forms at the dawn of the day. The voices in my head at times sang hymns with a tender melody; those songs would heal a troubled soul at a canter and melt a heart of stone without batting an eyelid.

At other times it broke things, minuscule things, and the not so petite. There are days the voices hold me by the jugular and lead me astray to dark places. I run a marathon with no finish line. I become a caricature. I fold and wilt under the weight of expectations. I consume silence as an overdose, hiding away my truth.

ADERAYO AND HER PHILANDERING SPOUSE

In the city where I grew up, we spoke about depression in hushed tones. We wore our depression under our skin like a road screaming no entry. I told this to Adam, a new-found acquaintance after Shindara walked away. Adam had lived in Australia all his life and had just arrived in Nigeria on a research study when we met. I discovered that we both had a flair for mental health and general wellbeing of those who were dear to our hearts. My tales bewildered Adam.

Adam's facial expression was worrisome. It reminded me of the concoction rice I used to cook during my Undergraduate days where the rice and tomato paste looked like they were sparring. "You mean you are not allowed to tell anyone about your pain?" Adam asked.

I explained that depression and mental health are alien to our society. You could call it a white man's disease. It wore different labels and colorations depending on who built a home for it.

I once told my father how I felt suicidal and he recommended taking me to the left side of Yaba. It wasn't until years later that I found out it was home to the most fragile in our society. The stigma of sharing my pain with him earned me the moniker "Omo Yaba" and at other times he would knock me down with vile words with no thought for my mental health amid the verbal onslaught from his arsenal. He was skilled in the art of killing me, killing me slowly.

Adam interjected, "Mental health issues shouldn't be waved aside as if it doesn't matter. It's okay to feel overwhelmed, shackled and shattered. It's okay to cry, to be emotional and let those high walls of being superhuman down. I would have died if I didn't seek help when I had mental health issues. I think physical health is synonymous with being mentally sound."

"I couldn't agree with you more," I replied.

My sister Aderayo, concealed all her troubles behind heavy make-up that perpetually shielded the trauma from her never-ending tears. Her failing marriage cast a big shadow over her sanity.

You could perceive the authenticity of Aderayo's misery through her phone's WhatsApp updates and display pictures. The more her philandering spouse roamed the streets like a stray dog, the more her emotional turbulence ***peaked***. The pictures wailed, huffed and puffed while some others accepted it as their fate. She had been beguiled by semantics of opinionated friends. Words bearing semblance to '***no one can change a man***' and 'if he is truly *yours* he will find his way back home,' have daily been used to console her like a patient on prescription drugs.

Her diet was asymmetrical. Her self-worth crumbled like a pack of falling cards. The pressure from her in-laws cast a big shadow over their matrimony and she could not idly sit by while her life was in crisis.

She had been married for over a decade with no offspring in tow. If I had any children of my own, I would have allowed her to adopt one of them to assuage her fears for her waning years. Her in-laws have been threatening and hurling abuse at her with a barrage of unsavoury words because she failed to give them a grandchild. They continue to demand a child, even though all the thirteen hospitals she has been to have given her a clean bill of health. In our culture, it's a woman's fault if a couple is childless, the man is encouraged to marry a second wife, nobody gets to question him. She suffers from bouts of clinical depression and her health continues to deteriorate by the day.

Adam interjected with flailing arms as if those arms would salvage the situation, "That's a very archaic practice you know, when one gender is disadvantaged in what should be a union of two partners. Where is the love then?" he reverberated.

I reiterated in a voice that signified to Adam it's a lost cause. I think the issue is over expectations; we expect so much from people.

The last time I met Aderayo over lunch, I told her jokingly, "Pull yourself together and move past this phase of hopelessness." She looked at me in despondency, "I wish I could, I wish it was that simple."

WILLIAM, 1981 - 2019

IN THE WEEKS following my meeting with Adam, the locals was rife with news of the death of William, a young man who died in an apparent suicide. His suicide note affirmed that the weight of societal expectations and his inability to measure up, led to his death. As I went to pay my condolences, William's father admonished all the youths present with deep pain in his voice and a thudding heart like pestle landing on yam in a mortar. "My son's death is painful and a catastrophic end to a young man with a great future." His voice suddenly became gravelly as those words hit home.

A few days prior William was a present feature, with a very promising future, and now he is referred to in the past, as a body. The assembly of youths sat on the couch some staring at the floor, while others stared into the ceiling immersed in grief. You could smell the abundance of sorrow right from the hallway into the living room. As the neighbourhood partook in the gloom, you could feel it in the way the community came together in solidarity for a young man who passed away at the peak of his powers. In the seating area, William's picture hanging on the wall depicts a young man full of life, but his body was now gathering dust, like an unopened book on a shelf with only fading memories to clutch to. There would be a lacuna, a large void which will be hard to fill.

I wonder where William is, if he can see us, hear us and feel the deep pain piercing through our hearts. Is he resting in peace? Or roasting in pieces? What happens in the land of the dead? Do they sleep, eat fried rice and chicken and have progenies, do they dream, or do their spirits just wander about aimlessly thinking of what might have been? I was lost in thought until William's father's voice jolted me out of my reverie. He continued as if communing with strange beings "social media is not an accurate measurement of success, don't let anyone pressure and ascribe a false label of failure, that's an easy way to die young. Forget the hashtags and clout chasing, don't fake it deceiving the world you have made it." He continued like a teacher who won't stop until his students understood the point he was trying to drive home. Life could be a paradox, but never give up.

As nightfall approached, I quietly left as I had to return home before my father arrived after a long day's work. I was dispassionate about visiting a house of mourning, so I hated being the recipient of bad news. It threw me into a frenzy and palpitations of great proportions. How do I console a grieving relative, I would always say? Would my words be a soothing balm or open fresh wounds? Would it provide immense relief like Robb ointment applied on a sprained ankle or burn intensely like an Aboniki ointment when used for the same purpose? A million and one questions raced through my mind as I made my way back home.

THE BEAUTY OF THERAPY

THE NEXT DAY, I had agreed to meet up with my coursemate, Harold, at the University Cafeteria after our respective lectures. We were both studying for our master's degree at the prestigious University of Lagos. The rate of unemployment was so high in the country that even doctorate degree holders roamed the streets aimlessly in search of a job. Going back to school for a second degree did not guarantee a job; however, it will drastically reduce our chances of staying unemployed for a long period. Being productive was a sure way of staying sane and out of trouble, hence, we embraced higher education like a golden treasure.

Harold was one of two boys from his parents. Born to a family on the fringe of middle class, depending on the government in power they could relapse into the lower strata of the society. His elder brother Henry was an athlete who had always been a role model to Harold but was sparsely at home because of his many athletic commitments both home and abroad. I became close friends with Harold when his Father was transferred in his Investment banking job from the Federal Capital territory to Lagos City and we lived in the same neighbourhood. Since Harold's dad's assignment to the ever-chaotic commercial Capital city began, their family life has been a rollercoaster, without the love and affection of a mother to cater to the emotions of Harold, life has been a long hard road for him. With every turbulent wind faced by Harold's dad by his boss who has a sledgehammer and an armoury of demeaning words to prey upon colleagues irrespective of years of experience, Harold's life became unbearable. His dad transferred all the aggression at him without batting an eye. After the semester break when Harold's results did not meet up to expectations, all hell let loose as his father brought out the comparison table. "You're just a waste of resources, your friend Adetayo keeps trailblazing your class and you're just here eating my food and drawing from the streams of mediocrity." Harold could smell fury, life in the commercial capital was turning into capital punishment as he has seen his father in beast mode. He remembered boasting to friends in his teenage years that his father couldn't hurt a fly; he would always say he was the best dad in the World. Apart from killing house flies that fly around without permission in their family home, day by day his father's words were killing him, like a poisonous trap sapping him of his energy and the essence of living.

In the weeks that followed, Harold became a recluse, like a snail retreating into his shell. The only difference was that Harold's shell is now cracked, splintered from words ripping his world into pieces.

As I met with Harold at the University cafeteria, he unburdened all his trauma and unending pain to me, 'a friend with a listening ear.' I earned that deserved appellation after I learned that one of the best ways to keep people on your side is the skill to listen to their problems and rightly so, I have become so adept at this, no one can contest that with me. Everyone needs a friend who they can confide in without throwing us under the bus and being judgmental. Harold bared his soul without mincing words to me, he told me of his fears, pain, and the deluge of abuse he has suffered since their relocation and his fathers' torrid time in the hell chamber called the 'Investment Bank.' I proclaimed, "I honestly believe that you and your father both will need to see a therapist." We need to quench this heat before it turns into a full-blown fire and consumes you both. Harold laughed hysterically, "I'm sorry for laughing this hard," he chirped like an angry bird who has just being let loose from a cage and somehow stumbled on his happy notes.

"Adetayo, you know what, where I come from it's a sign of weakness to see a therapist, counsellor, or whatever name you call it. We mask our pain; we pretend to be mentally strong and use our physical attributes as a shield. I can imagine the telling off I will get from my dad when I mention this to him."

My body went cold, this was my plan being thrown out of the window by Harold before he even gave it a chance to be watered, germinate and bear good fruits. I interrupted Harold, stuttering, "I have a great plan. What if you see the therapist first, and we can progress things from there?" Harold beamed with a smile that had a semblance to a coat of many colours, "sounds like a great plan my dear brother, thanks for always having my back."

I booked an appointment to see the therapist, paid the consultation fees out of my monthly allowance and ensured Harold arrived in time for what seems to be the road to redemption for my *'adopted brother'* as I would normally call him. The bond we shared transcends words on paper. I knew the benefit of therapy and the healing that comes with it. I sat in the reception area while Harold took a walk, he trudged on with wonky steps and a heavy heart. He knows this is a blank cheque to make magic happen, not just for himself but for his Dad as well; and he aims to make the best use of this thirty minutes consultation with the therapist.

As he shut the door behind him, all his worries, the weight of burden and the baggage of angst towards his dad, shut forever. After thirty minutes of unburdening and being soothed by words of healing, Harold walked out a new man like a newly baptized Christian who is ready for a brand-new start. He hugged me in a tight embrace, "this is what I have always needed, I promise you my Dad will come here, he will be here for real."

On a bright sunny afternoon during the summer holidays, Harold's Dad walked through the double doors to see the therapist. He had come alone after his new forged friendship with Harold resulting from the magic of therapy. He'd asked Harold, "what's the secret?" Harold waxed lyrical, "Dad it's therapy, I have a new lease on life thanks to therapy." "A problem shared is a problem half solved," he enthused with a beam as pronounced as the halogen beam that gives their back-garden light through the dark of night.

The morning after his holidays ended, Harold's Dad went to work with his resignation letter at hand, ready to give himself and his boys a fighting chance at getting the best of him. He knocked on the Chairman's door, ready to pack it all up. Chief Olayiwola, the Chairman, welcomed him with a smile that told more than a thousand stories. "I hope no one has told you this, this is my news to break, and it's your time to giggle and have the last laugh," he enthused with a smile that hid his brown teeth discoloured by his love for *kolanuts*. "Congratulations Mr. Okechukwu Madumere the new managing Director of Future King Securities Inc."

As I reminisce about the events of the past months, I wrap my mind around the notion that mental health shouldn't be pushed aside. Everyone has a baggage of problems they tend to, sowing seeds of kindness and love can heal a troubled soul.

INFERNO OF SILENCE

Kunle dropped his bag on the dining table. The table was starting to creak from all the unplanned baggage it silently bore. He enjoyed taking the ferry a few minutes from his office. Not only did it afford him a few minutes of silence before his wife got home, he also enjoyed the view from the boat. He especially liked watching in the far distance, the ships berthing at Apapa ports, swaying on the waves of the sea.

He liked to think that he bore the weight of his problems on his shoulder like the ports bore the weight of the ships. But he was not the sea, he did not bear the load on his shoulder so gracefully. He was a man, a man whose wife evoked unfamiliar emotions within him. He had tried to discuss this with his father. Once, his father had waved away his concerns, in the process his hands waving away the smoke from his tobacco towards the east. "All women are crazy," he had said, "you just have to know how to handle them."

Handle not like a mother 'handled' a child, but more like how a Nigerian soldier 'handled' a belligerent *danfo* driver or how some women 'handled' the devil they believed possessed a slow housemaid. He did not like this type of handling; in fact it repulsed him. He had watched his father punch his mother into submission and he had vowed never to be that man; and now that his father was emphasising it, he blamed himself for seeking marital advice from a man he detested in the first instance.

He had briefly considered asking their Pastor for advice, but he had been deeply troubled that the man would think him unfit to be a husband. After all, on their wedding day, he had admonished Kunle to firmly steer his household in the right direction. Would the Pastor now consider him weak, a sham of a man after the long episodes of marriage counselling they had gone through before saying 'I do.'

He still remembered their wedding day so clearly. Sometimes he shuddered at the thought that it would always mark the day he signed away his sanity.

He took a forlorn look at the wall and their wedding pictures stare back at him as if uttering in a sarcastic tone, "I told you." The pastor admonished him and

Adaeze on the altar before they took the vows, "Try to resolve your issues between you both and don't allow a third party to meddle in your affairs." This line sounded like a habitual ritual in the over fifty ceremonies he had attended in Victoria Garden city and its environs. How will he tell the pastor that the rumours of his squabble with the one they all call '*Mama*' was discussed at the Newspaper stand the other day in the mouth of strangers and Akara chewing Okada riders?

He still remembers the apathetic faces of the wedding guests, that day, hiding their disgust at the prolonged rhetoric flowing from the pulpit. Most people were after the sumptuous meal which would be served at the reception party, or so he thought. But now, he thinks they were rather fed up as he is now with the same old message that outlines almost impossible marriage principles to abide by.

Don't hold grudges, settle your issues before the moon holds sway. Respect each other. Love without flinching and always remember that you're in this for the long haul. And keep this in your left hand '**God hates divorce**.' The pastor kept emphasizing the words with beads of sweat on his forehead and his white handkerchief now turning to a shade of brown. He and Adaeze occasionally exchanged glances at each word with the certainty that it was a walkover. But now, it feels like he is sitting on a hot seat solving an Algebraic equation he was never taught in school.

The memories of the first day he met Adaeze were vivid in his heart. It was on a Thursday morning when the oil tankers caused the usual traffic gridlock that was now part of his daily commute. He was running late for his routine medical check-up with Dr. Adekogbe, the General Practitioner at the General Hospital Apapa. As he walked into the hospital, dejection was boldly written on his face at the thought he had missed his appointment. A stranger sporting a white uniform walked up to him, her warm smile calming his frayed nerves.

"You look worried sir; how can I help you?" she said.

"I have an appointment with Dr. Adekogbe, which I think I have missed," he replied.

"Hold on sir, while I check for you," she said walking briskly towards the doctor's office.

In a flash, she beckoned towards him, "You're so lucky, the next patient is still not here," she said, her gap teeth visible as she smiled.

"Thank you so much for your help today," he said, the worry on his face now a distant memory.

The GP Dr. Adekogbe is as old as the hospital furniture; she had received *five* different state governors to the hospital. "Meet Adaeze, our new nursing assistant," Dr. Adekogbe said.

"Oh I guessed as much, the face looked unfamiliar," Kunle said, extending his hand.

"You're welcome to the hospital," he told her in a tone that made her feel welcome.

"Pleased to meet you Sir," she said in an accent that sounded neither foreign nor Igbo.

At the end of his appointment, in the reception area his eyes met hers as she made way to escape the evening traffic. "Do you drive, if not I can drop you off?" he said.

"Thanks for the offer but I can always find my way," she said. As far as she was concerned, he was a stranger and her mother's words continued to haunt her 'beware of strange men' she would say.

"Let me do the honours just this time," he said pleading.

"Okay," just one ride won't hurt, she thought to herself as she stepped into the car.

On the drive home, she exuded innocence, she rarely spoke and when she did, her words were few and sounded gentle. As he waved her off, he slid his business card into her palms.

"Come around tomorrow evening to my office since it's your day off," he said, then watched her enter her apartment before he zoomed off.

* * * * *

His diary for the day was the same as last week when he suffered a burn-out.

As the mounting appointments dissipated, he heard a knock on the door. Standing in for the boss while away to Disneyland had its own perks: sole access to a secluded meeting room, the luxury of a complimentary car, and the grudging respect from his colleagues. But the countless back to back meetings made him grow weary. Few weeks ago, his boss, Mr. Oshikoya had complained of stress. He laughed in hysterics when telling their other colleagues how *'stressed'* their big boss was and they all grumbled and murmured and craved for that kind of stress. A big man's stress is better than being an *office worker* with nothing tangible to show for the stress, they concluded. Now, as he sat on Mr. Oshikoya's seat, every evening he would stare at the calendar fervently praying for him to be back earlier than scheduled.

"Come on in," he said, not looking up from his laptop.

She walked in and said in a calming voice, "I trust your day has been great."

"Not so bad," he said, his facial expression showing a mixture of weariness and delight at seeing her. She was now seated on the empty plastic chair.

"Let's go out on the town tonight, considering you're new here," he said, breaking the awkward silence that had overshadowed the room.

"That would be brilliant." her face breaking into a bubble of delight.

After their first day in town, they struck an intimate friendship and she began to leave her personal belongings in the one-bedroom apartment which he termed his *resting place*. First, it was her nightgowns that were folded neatly into his wardrobe, before her small luggage box found refuge beside the iron table and in three months, her room had become vacant.

On the night she brought her last *Ghana must go* bag to his room where they barely had space to walk in without colliding into bags. "Why not give up your flat now that you have moved in with me?" he said in a suggestive tone that indicated that was the most logical thing to do. She replied, "I would like to keep it, as a fall-back option. You know, men have the tendency to misbehave when they see a woman has no alternative. Please allow me to keep it; I will continue to pay for it. If that's what you want," she said in a persuasive tone even though she had made up her mind.

He said nothing.

The next week after Adaeze made his abode home, the house began to have a semblance of sanity. He could feel Adaeze's touch in the way she organised things around the house. Even the drinking glass cups looked different as they were decked on new trays.

Exactly three months after Adaeze moved in, he popped the question he sensed she had been longing for, *will you marry me?* With his knees buried in the sand at Oniru beach. Adaeze was overwhelmed with emotions, tears streaming down her face. She buried her face in his chest and echoed in a gentle voice, "you're my dream come true."

As the wedding preparations drew near, he had noticed Adaeze raised her voice while they were discussing the choice of colour for Aso-ebi. He had jokingly suggested blue instead of the pink she wanted. He said still light-hearted, "you chose the reception venue, vendors, decorators, and caterers, why can't you leave the Aso ebi for me to choose? Or don't you think my voice deserves to be heard."

She walked out of the room without uttering a word, slamming the door on his face.

He had waved it off saying this was out of character for her. Weeks after, Adaeze began to vent on how he had left his wet towel on the bed, she would also whinge on how disorganised he was.

"You can't just do anything right," she would say. He wanted to talk but he couldn't bear to utter the words as his mouth felt heavy.

He began to shudder at the thought of the marriage. Exactly two days before the wedding, he held his face on his palm for destroying the zipper to her bridal gown. He simply walked out of the house, the cool breeze caressing his swollen face.

Immediately after the honeymoon the tide of abuse continued unabated. Adaeze complained about how small the new house was, the old curtains, the unkempt garden and she wore her fury on her face. He would always escape through the front door before she unleashed the venom in her tongue.

He remembers vividly the day his colleagues were chitchatting at work. Their office fondly called the 'Oval Office' because they were deemed the nerve centre of the organisation. He sat in a position in the centre, which made it easy for his eyes to dart around the office effortlessly. The conversation that day was sparked by 'Hauwa' the office gist starter after their boss walked towards the meeting room clutching his files.

Hmmmn uhm, "can you imagine what I just saw?" Hauwa said. "Tell us o," Rolake replied with her ears itching to hear the gist. Hauwa continued, "it's a thread on twitter about a woman who beat her husband to a pulp." The voices of the three other male colleagues Nnamdi, Rauf and Emeka were now pitch high.

He could hear words that pricked at him, and he began to fidget on his seat.

"No woman can try that with me, that's unacceptable," as they kept discussing the subject matter.

"What kind of rubbish love is that?" Rauf said, asking no one in particular. Rolake spoke next about how it was an abomination for a true African Queen to beat up her king. Then Emeka noticing his quiet demeanour asked, "Kunle, what is your opinion about this madness in the name of love?"

He could only nod his head, pretending to be immersed in the files scattered on his table.

Nnamdi had said he couldn't even imagine his wife saying no to sex. If only they knew he would give up sex for the rest of his life in exchange for quietness. Sometimes he found himself daydreaming his wife had an accident that would claim her 'larynx.'

Six months into their wedding, he arrived at the office on a Friday morning and found a strange letter on his desk. He tried to gauge the mood in the office that morning, but everyone kept a straight face. He had opened the letter with trembling hands and immediately he saw the subject. His mood went sour. He only had ten minutes to exit the building and hurriedly said his goodbye packing his most treasured belongings.

The company had laid off two hundred staff and he was caught in the panic. He was the only one that was axed in the 'Oval Office.' Shock and great disbelief pervaded the atmosphere. In the corridors, colleagues spoke in whispers. If Kunle who delivered the *best numbers* could be let go, then no one is safe here, they said. On the way home, he had a chilling feeling about it and his head swivelled in a whirlwind of emotions.

"You look like a beaten man," she said perfectly capturing his mood.

He sunk into a sofa and said in a shaky voice, "I have been stripped naked by a company I gave my all to."

She wrapped her arms around him and said in a loving voice, "tomorrow will birth possibilities."

His quest to get back to the nine-to-five routine constantly met a brick wall. The slush of emails with, unfortunately you have not been selected on this occasion in the body, always set him in a mood. As the months went by, he began to lose his sense of self-worth. She began to resent him, the sight of him floating around the house infuriated her.

"You're not pushy, you're not doing enough to get back on the job market," she thundered in a loud voice. The words hit him hard and left him dazed. He wasn't sure if he heard her or his mind held him captive. "Ada don't tell me you do not appreciate all my effort to assume responsibility for this family, our family." He threw her pet name in the mix hoping that might soften her stance. Her arms now folded across her chest. "Kunle, I'm sorry to burst your bubble, show me your offer letter and I will forever maintain my peace." Her words felt like a piercing arrow; from her body language he could tell he had lost the battle.

In the weeks that followed, he grieved and cried silent tears at the demise of their once happy union. Once, he had tried to initiate foreplay to rekindle their failing love. As he ran his fingers on her navel, she jerked, surprise written all over her and uttered disinterested '*a man without money is not permitted to have an erection.*' Through the night, her words haunted him casting a shadow over his bubbling spirit.

Before the sun shone through the windows, Adaeze catwalks into the parlour to pick up her purse. She's dressed gorgeously and he is tempted to admire but he remembers there's an invisible wall between them that she won't allow him to demolish. He watches her walk through the door and shut it without saying a word. He knows she will open it again, pop in her head and throw out a sentence. It's her way of quenching the guilt that surges in her when she leaves him without an idea where she's heading to.

The door opens and he sees her braids fall through, then her neatly carved eyebrows, and then, her full-face popping through the door.

"Just want to dash down to town." That's all she says and retrieves her head. He doesn't even have a chance to nod or smile, let alone throw a kiss and say goodbye.

Mentally exhausted, he reaches for his laptop lying on the centre table. He types some obscure words into google search engine.

In their society, they build men to be steely, to withstand all weather. After all men will always be men; men shouldn't wilt no matter what's thrown at them.

He is trying to be that man. He is trying not to be the type that social media is awash with. The ones who trap their women with a hail of abhorrent words and heavy blows. Men who can't fight to save their lives but prey on their wives and girlfriends as if it's the latest craze in town. It reminds him of Cornelius, his friend, who batters his wife, but they make out in bed afterward. He always wonders why she finds it hard to walk away. He was told she is a Liverpool fan and lives by the mantra: You will never walk alone.

In a bid to be the yardstick for other husbands, he expires in silence as he is worn out emotionally. He is trying hard to keep to the pastor's sermon, "Try to resolve your issues between you both and don't let a third party meddle in your affairs." But Mama Nosa, the noisey, nosey neighbour, won't let him be. She is the type of neighbour always in need of salt and Maggi. All to poke her nose in wetin no concern her. She chinwags and natters with the other neighbours until time passes them by. Mama Nosa always finds joy amid negativity and confusion. That is an inkling that she would always have something to chatter about. Her behaviour is abhorrent and turns him off. Last weekend, he went to the shopping mall and bought a beautiful artwork that screamed in loud terms "MIND YOUR BUSINESS." He hung it on the wall in a conspicuous place so Mama Nosa could see it. She did come again to ask for a mop bucket, but he hasn't seen her after then, nor had he heard of her need for salt or Maggi or to say her usual halfhearted good morning which disappeared with the evening moon.

His phone beeps in his pocket and he pulls it out to check. He peers at the screen with a pair of eyes surrounded by eye pockets resulting from stored up tears and late-night thinking. It's a message from Adaeze that reads: 'Won't be home tonight. Catch you in the morning before I go to work.' He shuts his eyes and exhales loudly, feeling his eye pockets sag from yet another stored-up tear. Once again, he would sleep on a king size bed alone. He is starting to get used to it. After all, even when she is there, he clutches his pillow like it's his second wife.

His marriage to Adaeze reminds him of his father's first Volkswagen Beetle. It was a one in a town kind of car. Not for any grand aesthetics or design, children in the area nicknamed the car "patch-patch" because of its torn seats that were held together by threads that were parting like the red sea. He knows deep down that his love affair with Adaeze is on the brink, hanging loosely by a thread just like his father's car seats.

During the summer months, Adaeze and he were engrossed in a bitter argument when they heard a knock on the door. He put up a smiling face as he opened the door, with the hope that Adaeze would do the same. Gratefully, she withdrew into the bedroom. Bamidele, his friend from the United Kingdom, came in with another friend of his whom neither him nor Adaeze knew. He was about to throw Bamidele a hug when Adaeze's voice came on like a loudspeaker.

"You this lazy man! You're entertaining friends when you are jobless and penniless." She ranted at the top of her voice from the inner recesses of the main bedroom. She ripped him into pieces then she swore at him and cursed the day she met him. The foul stench from her mouth pervaded the whole atmosphere. She had always believed that issues could only be settled when human bodies were set on fire.

"Let me tell you Kunle, I am a feminist. I know my rights." Still brimming with anger.

He listened to her quote feminism like it was all about opposing and fighting the male counterpart. He swept the little hairs that jotted out of his scalp backward and muttered, "You're an extremist, not a feminist," in whispers. His dirty linens were not just washed in public, they were sun-dried and left for the whole-world to cast derisory glances at.

He put up a brave face; two wrongs never make a right. The stranger chuckled. He saw him grin and dead silence enveloped the room as he gazed at him forlornly with a look of a wailer skilled in the art of pity-parties. He could hear the stranger's spittle passing through his throat like a faulty tap which just found its rhythm.

Bamidele has also had his fair share of marital woes. He was rendered homeless and barred from seeing his children while he lived in the United Kingdom. He had a failed marriage, but was lucky to have come out of it thriving. Many of his contemporaries could not share their bitter tales before the inferno of silence consumed them.

Kunle was livid with rage. He could feel his intestines crawl in disgust. He swallowed the anger in a flash before the anger swallowed him and he found himself in police trouble and a life of unending sorrow. He was going to be the loser, so he played it safe. He quenched the desire to shout, throw a fist, or brawl. Thankfully, Bamidele suggested they all go to the bar to grab a glass.

He could hear Adaeze yell, "Fool!" as they drove away. He is glad he played the fool so he can remain on the queue of few good men.

Bamidele drove the car down to the bar as he was in disarray. Kunle exhaled loudly as Bamidele revved the car at breakneck speed, as he had felt uneasy being around the stranger, whom he later knew as Lasisi.

As they arrived at the bar, Bamidele said, "I can see you are in turmoil, I will leave you now to pull it together," as he headed for the dance floor with Lasisi. At the bar, he sat in a corner struggling to drink his way out of the lingering problem that cast a shadow over his matrimony. The one bottle of Guinness extra stout he drank halfway left a bitter taste in his mouth. "What are you doing here by yourself?" a husky voice jolted him out of his musing. It was Anthony, his roommate at the University of Lagos. He hadn't changed much from the days they were united by books and their love for everything academic, apart from his protruding belly. The six bottles of Heineken lying empty across his table told the whole story. At the University he was his confidante, he couldn't keep his mouth shut, bearing all his hurt to Anthony as if he had a magic wand. "I can relate with your troubles," Anthony stated emphatically as if they were both boarded in the same ship of marital woes. "Kunle, I have had my fair share of affliction," he sounded pained. "I was raped and lost my virginity to my girlfriend; to date no one believes me. Men cannot be raped, you're lying was the constant hogwash thrown my way. And my marriage only lasted for six months as the woman I called darling beats me up for fun." Kunle's mouth flung open in bewilderment, as no one would believe his tales either.

Anthony continued, "How can she beat you? Are you not a man? Was the response I received from everyone who found the courage to reply whenever I had the courage to share the hell of a life, I had with Atinuke. It was as if everyone else expected me to beat her up in retaliation to show my masculinity. Some others would just shake their head in pity, with their mouths too heavy to utter a word."

He left the bar for home, with no solution to his problems in sight.

When his friends ask him, "Kunle how do you feel?" He takes a deep breath. He does not reply with "I feel terrible" or "I'm hurting" because he is not supposed to. He is a man. He is built to feel zero pain. *Real men don't cry.*

He wondered where he had gone wrong with this marriage business, where his sweet Adaeze went.

How did she become this bitter black belt holder who unleashed the whip as she pleased and how he had inadvertently purchased bazaar goods by choosing to marry her. This question kept him awake late into the night, sometimes early morning, and left him communing with strange beings at odd hours.

His dose of medications included silent treatment, a cold shoulder, and the nagging wife syndrome in no fitting order. There were weeks the inferno of silence, hard core malice and repetitive fits of anger consumed him. Over time, he had developed a coping mechanism to live peacefully with Adaeze: be subservient, say the right things, and never ask her to repeat herself. Adaeze hates repetitive questions; they sent her off a cliff, drive her into a rage, and release a bolt of inbuilt anger. She is a definition of impatience, so he must always be on his best behaviour, wearing it like a perfume that doesn't wear out.

Their honeymoon in Dubai was still vivid in his memory. It was the first time he saw Adaeze take off her mask, since they got married. He had enjoyed some sort of serenity since their wedding day till they arrived in Dubai. In the early months of their courtship, she had been the angel that never reacted even when a sword is thrust into her. That day, she told him in a tone that set fire to human bodies after her anger button was detonated, "You mean you will not upload our wedding pictures to your Instagram page? Or is there anything you are hiding from me?" Stillness overshadowed their room, save for the tick-tock of the exquisite clock mounted on the wall of their room. He was exasperated but tried his very best to mask it. He had close pals who uploaded pictures of their wedding which they later had to delete when their marriages hit the rocks. He would rather not be put through the agony of face-saving; hence, his obdurate stance.

Jadesola, his childhood friend, was a classic example. She was smitten in love with Obinna, her fiancé of three years. She uploaded their honeymoon pictures on Twitter which set the internet on wildfire and it was the same pictures that acted as the fuel that engulfed their marriage before it got started. The drama that would devour her infant nuptial begun from an innocent hashtag #besthusbandever that went viral after singles from far and near coveted their union. After some other ladies recognized Obinna for who he truly was, a second hashtag trended #fatherabraham. Obinna was a father of many sons and it took an innocent picture to expose him as the father of six boys from six different women. He had a plethora of baby mamas. He was a reputable sperm donor who was also a motivational speaker and entrapped spinsters in his web of deceit with his sugar-coated tongue. Jadesola had been bitten by the one she thought would be her prince charming. She was within touching distance of self-harm after the incident and years later, she has found it difficult to love and give her heart freely to any man. She would say, "Men can't be trusted." He recounted the story to Adaeze for the umpteenth time, but she was having none of it.

"Are you insinuating that this marriage will hit the rocks, or that I am hiding something from you?" she charged at him like a rampaging bulldog.

There is an inferno; he is the victim set on fire by the woman who swore to love and cherish him till death comes knocking. He is burning, like unattended asun meat left to cook by a wandering seller.

He went to his big uncle, who was a father figure, to discuss his predicament eleven months into their matrimony. Uncle Adeleke was a tough and no-nonsense man. He had always confided in him throughout his teenage years and nothing seemed to have changed over the years. He enlisted in the army in his early twenties and has since risen to the acme of his career. Uncle Adeleke charged him to man up. He barked like a commander leading a battalion to the war front.

"Kunle, don't be weak. Don't allow any woman to press your *mumu button* and turn you into a lightweight." He replied to his uncle calmly. He had always been smooth and sleek right from his University days. "Uncle you know that fire for fire will only lead to a full-blown war. I would prefer to tread cautiously and use native intelligence instead."

Not long after the visit, news of his marital woes travelled faster than a high-speed train. He vowed to follow the pastor's advice to the letter. He would rather be buried in the inferno of silence than allow his muddle to be concealed in the tongue of strangers and friends in equal measure.

He is still on the hunt for the Adaeze he dated for six months before their wedding. It feels like a missing persons alert and it's turning scary. Maybe he should have courted her for more than six months. He thinks they didn't spend enough time in the relationship to know each other better. Then, his mind raced to Paulina, who dated Arewa for six years and their matrimony only lasted six weeks.

Two years and ten months into their marriage, Adaeze's pandora box of sleazy affairs unravelled at a canter unbeknownst to her. His inability to fend for the family had made him a lightweight. He saw himself as a pawn in this game. He remembered their first meeting vividly. He built conjectures in his mind about heaven on earth. This was his forever happily ever after. He had always envisioned a perfect union, made in heaven and the envy of people. On that day, as he exchanged pleasantries, there was a chemistry and they struck a chord. It had only ended up in a marriage with upheavals, an emotional rollercoaster, seasoned with vile words and a trail of abuse.

The night had come meeting him in the same position as he was when Adaeze left. He is fagged out, not from work or any other activity, but from this marriage.

"I will give one more try tomorrow when she returns," he soliloquized.

Adaeze is back. He spreads his arms open to receive her in an effort to rekindle a tiny spark of their old flame. They laugh together and eat before she recoils into her space. He flips through channels on the TV before he mounts the bed to see if Adaeze will be in the mood for bonking. It's been three long months since the creaking sound on the wooden bed had been heard. Even the wooden bed should be aware all is not well between them. Sexual intimacy no longer features in their agenda, as he had been trapped by one excuse after the other. Mood, tiredness, and anything Adaeze can conjure to avoid sex. Adaeze says in a hostile voice, "I'm not in the mood for all this right now. I have a few hours to sleep before I arise and prepare for work." He says nothing in reply.

Everything has an end. A week after, he takes a walk never to be seen again.

RETURN JOURNEY

"Hard to find a fine boy who's not a fuck boy," Richard Brady, the famous on-air personality on Metro Radio, joked.

Ade dismissed the voice and turned off the knob of his car radio. He took a reverse as directed by the uniformed man standing in front of his Avensis in the car park, moving here and there till he was parked properly. The Lowry Hotel was right before him and he paused to admire the tall, elegant structure. Manchester billionaires and business moguls struck multi-billion-pound deals here. His dimples shone with a glint of satisfaction, delighted to be one of those who would strike a business deal at the Lowry Hotel, today.

Beep. Beep. Beep. It was his mobile phone. He allowed it to ring for a few seconds as customary before answering the call, and partly because he believed his dad was the caller. A few minutes earlier, he was in a gentle scuffle with him on the phone over the topic he dreaded to discuss with his parents the most.

"Son, when will you stop philandering with women and settle down?" his father had queried. "Your mother and I are not getting any younger."

He believed he had already given his father a piece of his mind, so he let the call ring through till it ended before heading out of his car for the magnificent building. He was in no mood for another round of argument. As he entered, he made a dash for the *gents* for a last-minute check on his appearance. He gave thumbs up to the mirror as a heartfelt thank you and his cheekbones glowed like bright rays of the afternoon sun.

Sauntering off into the lobby and towards the elevator, his eyes met with a brown skin beauty in wait for it as well. For a moment, he thought he had seen Miriam. He blinked and 'unblinked' before realising she wasn't the one. The lady's eyes were transfixed on his glowing dark skin in admiration as he drew closer. She lifted her eyes to his head, observing his clean skin-cut, and then to his horse moustache. He mouthed a good morning taking a stand by her but rather than get a reply, he got a silent *woosh!* and a suck of air into her mouth as if she was imagining having a romantic moment with him. The pinkness of his lips had her thrilled. Such incidents no longer amused him. He got advances from women, old and young, on a daily basis. Sometimes, he seized the opportunity to catch a fish. Other times, like today, he let it go.

The elevator opened and they walked in quietly, trying hard not to look into each other's eyes. Her eyes lowered to his jacket pocket as she spotted bright light flashing through. It was his phone vibrating but several seconds after, he was yet to make a move to pull it out.

"You've got a call," she said curiously.

At first, he nodded and smiled lightly without any intention of picking the call but a look at her curious eyes made him change his mind. He pulled out the phone and without checking the caller, said, "Dad," with an air of exasperation. Jake was at the other end of the line.

"Oh, I'm sorry." He was slightly embarrassed. Jake was checking in to see if the meeting would start in thirty minutes as planned and to be sure Ade was not one who worked on the 'African time.' Ade nodded in affirmation and answered coolly, "Yes, that was the plan." He was a stickler for time and always ensured he arrived at least forty minutes early for all meetings, so he could have adequate time to reflect and crosscheck his meeting notes. Today was his big day too, and being late would ruin the efforts he had put in to come up with the perfect pitch that would please his Capitalist Investors.

He recalled the day he sighted Jake at a breakfast meeting in Whitehall, London, he called a miracle day. While he was busy thinking of how he would catch up with the famous CEO of Future Heir Capital, Jake had turned back and headed for the elevator in his direction to pick up his phone which he had forgotten on his seat at the meeting. Ade followed him and took the same elevator where he finally had a one-on-one brief chat with him.

The brown skin beauty brushed Ade as she walked past him out of the elevator into the executive lounge. He looked sideways into his pocket, sensing she had done something spooky. He was right. A blue call card was in his pocket. He picked it and turned it over to the other side. There was a short note that read, "Call me." Flirting wasn't on his agenda today, so he returned the card to his pocket without keen interest.

"Gentleman, what would you like to drink?" A waiter sporting an all-white ensemble asked as Ade took a seat by a table.

"Hot water," he retorted.

The waiter's wide smile quickly faded into a frown. He silently mused to himself, 'Who drinks hot water at the Lowry?' Ade, sensing his disdain, echoed, "My choice, my business."

The waiter served the hot water smiling like he had forgotten the past altercation between them. These theatrics, too, were not new to Ade. *The customer would always be right and feted like royalty; that is the one and only way to earn a good tip.* He sipped gently on the teacup. His love affair with hot water started as a teenager and he would constantly remind anyone who cared to listen that that was the secret to his glowing skin and good looks.

There was an expensive mirror half-way up the wall, opposite Ade. He was tall enough to stretch only a little in order to take one more look at himself. Tracey, Jake's business partner and good friend was coming along, so he needed to be sure he was spotless just in case she was another chick he could catch. He smiled at the thought of having a fling with one of his prospective investors and for a moment, imagined her in bed with him, having a swell time. Soon, his imaginations took a different turn. Rather than Tracey, he started to see Miriam in his arms, pulling at his lips with hers so passionately that he felt his body move in reaction and he had to look around to be sure no one noticed.

Resting his back against the chair, he recalled the first time he set eyes on Miriam. Her glowing brown skin in the thick fur coat she wore was the first thing that caught his eyes. She was in a chitchat with her Chinese friend at the Social Science faculty sign post of Cambridge University when he drove past in his salon car, splashing water at her.

"I'm sorry, I wasn't looking," he apologised.

"Apology unaccepted. Are you nuts? Can't you see the wet ground?" She looked deep into his eyes, unsmiling. He opened his mouth to say something but the look of displeasure on her face and the way she narrowed her eyes as if willing to attack him further if he attempted defending himself, muted him.

"That's okay," the Chinese cut in. "We're running late for our class." She placed her hand at Miriam's back and led her inside the faculty while Ade looked on a little amazed at her reaction. Splashing water on her was unintentional but he had also wrongly presumed it was his perfect chance to meet a new chick. With the ladies out of sight, he zapped off to his faculty. He was also running late for his class but if Miriam had been receptive, he would have ignored the lecture for a chat with her. As he walked into his faculty reception, he chuckled at the thought that it took the splash of water to remind the ladies of their lecture. *Girls and gossip*, he mumbled.

"Excuse me?" Tracey shifted her face halfway to her side while maintaining her gaze on him. She was in a Gucci shirt on a blue skirt clutching her customary designer handbag, Jake by her side.

"Oh wow! Umm…I…sorry." He bit his tongue, pissed at his stutter. A sudden nervousness swept down his spine at the sight of the British capitalist investors standing before him in sleek outfits.

"It's fine, Ade," Jake eased, his hand stretched forward for a shake. His pronunciation of Ade sounded like *aduh* with a fall on the second syllable. Ade seized his hand in a quick dash, pulling him down a little.

"I'm sorry. I'm sorry," he apologised again.

"Just try not to be sorry again." Jake's face was straight this time. He withdrew his hand to his three-piece suit which Ade imagined would have set him back a few thousand bucks, and pulled out a handkerchief for a clean. Ade lifted his eyes slightly, creating folds on his forehead. *OCD or habit?* he pondered and let the thought slide. He too, was a neat freak except that he wouldn't embarrass his guests with it. He made for a mild, formal hug with Tracey but she turned aside politely towards the direction of the presentation space they had booked for the meeting. The smirk on her face didn't go unnoticed.

The temperature of the meeting room was cooler than the executive lounge but Ade found it hot. His nerves were yet to be calm, making everything around feel hot. They were quietly seated around a table, watching the waitress serve their various drink preferences and waiting for her to leave. Ade cast a glance at her smooth, straight legs in her green mini skirt. Miriam's straight legs strapped around his waist, with her butt dancing in his palms as he leaned against the wall of his apartment, flashed through his mind briefly. He took off his eyes quickly before the waitress turned round and headed for the exit.

"Jake educated me about you and your business idea but I did my personal research as well," Tracey began, "and I must say, I'm quite impressed." Her accent was clear and polished, and her touch of class mixed with simplicity amused and impressed Ade. He fancied these types of ladies. Miriam was the only lady he dated who was less of the class and style his exes were.

"Course and Research Leader, Cambridge University. Best Graduating Student, Management Information Systems Department, Cambridge University. Winner, Manchester University Innovator Prize."

Ade stroked his beard listening to Tracey reel out his achievements. His confidence was starting to spring up again and he was sure now that he could handle the pitch when it began.

"But what startles me is the National Poetry Competition Prize." She narrowed her eyes at him. "Kindly tell, how did the CEO of New Wave Tech Hub receive a poetry prize?"

Ade's love for writing had been on for as long as he could remember, and books were his way of relaxing and calming his frayed nerves. On one of such days, when he was sitting on a street bench by a restaurant reading Idanre and Other Poems, his favourite poetry collection by Wole Soyinka, he heard a voice say, "I see we are fans of the same poet." He shut the book immediately and looked up to see Miriam standing before him in a leather jacket, blue jeans and a pair of boots shielding her feet from the snowy ground. That was the fourth time in a year they had run into each other. Each time he struggled to engage her in a conversation but she was brash in her responses and left quickly. This time around, she started the conversation and he knew it was his chance to make something happen.

"Call me Miriam," she said with her hands in her jeans pocket as she took a seat by him.

"I'm Ade," he replied, breathing heavily. He was surprised at her sudden friendliness after giving up on trying to get her to talk to him. She seemed lively and excited about something he had no idea about.

"Today's my birthday and I decided to be nice to everyone I come across."

I decided to be nice... Ade got caught up in laughter. Miriam joined him. Their laughter was loud enough to disturb the peace of the people sitting by, but they cared less.

"That means you're not always nice."

"Something like that. And I will be nicer to you if you let me go home with the book in your hand." Miriam winked at him and flashed her perfect set of teeth so white that Ade was taken aback. He knew she was pretty but he had never imagined her this beautiful. Without waiting to hear his response, she took the book from him and said, "Let me have your number. I'll call you as soon as I'm through with it." Ade blinked. Such guts! He called out his number and watched her punch the keys on her phone screen with her long, pink painted nails. She was gorgeous but far from classy like Emmy the Carribean, Lucy the daughter of a British Major General, Jane the American Mayor's niece, and the rest of the women he'd had in his life, yet, she raptured him with everything about her. As she walked away from him into the restaurant, he stared at her, feeling excited about the little attention she had given him. He never knew that someday, a woman would make him crave her attention and almost beg for it. And he had always believed that even if it ever happened, it would be a woman who could stand in the place of a deity. He leaned back against the bench and swept his hand through his punk hairdo wondering why he felt the way he did for her. The vibration from his phone brought him back to the present. When he pulled out his phone to check the notification, it was a message from Miriam which read: *Your punk hairdo is cool but you'll look cuter in a skin-cut with a horse moustache.* He started to laugh but this time, quietly, suppressing the urge to let it out.

That night, he gathered all the books and diaries where he had written some of his composed poetry pieces. Now that he knew Miriam had a thing for poetry, he wanted to show her how much of a poet he was. He was desperate to impress her. In one of the diaries, he had scribbled a poem, *A Wobbly Descent*. At the top of the page, he had noted *Not too great. Discard.*

Hide the truth in a bubble wrap

Smoothen the greases

Our gazes are aloof

The language of our body is indifference

Your voice echoes in loud whispers

Feels crushed from this weight of despair

There are days you drown in a sea of lies

A mist covers your face like dark

clouds serenading the blue skyline.

You choke from the fumes of sorrow

that pervades the atmosphere.

Last week, truth was smothered and

deception surged as
rushing waters overflowing its bank.
Your tongue tilted the other way-
caught in a web of lies.
Truth looked on forlorn as deception
took the centre stage.

"I love love love this one!" Miriam exclaimed when she was done reading it. They were seated in the school library. Ade was spotting Miriam's recommended hairdo, which became his signature style no matter the pleas of his other exes after Miriam to try something new.

"You do?"

"Of course."

"I was thinking of discarding it."

"Don't you dare. You know what? The National Poetry Competition is ongoing right now. I'm sure you know about it already."

"Yeah, but…"

"No buts. I'm telling you it's great. As a poetry fanatic and critique, I can tell great poetry pieces when I see them. So, I'm asking you to submit this one. Besides, it fits into the submission guidelines of the contest."

Jake and Tracey smiled. "Love made you earn such a prestigious prize," Tracey said. "Nice story."

The smiles on their faces faded quickly as they put up expressions that read, *let's get back to business*. Ade straightened himself up on his seat and croaked his throat knowingly. Tracey flipped open the file before her on the table and scrutinised the details in it. Afterward, she lifted her eyes to him, looking him straight in the eye, 'unblinking.' He slowly shifted his eyeballs from her to Jake, and then to the file before him.

"So, you're considering opening a branch of New Wave Tech Hub in the metropolitan city of Lagos and you want Jake and I to partner with you," she said. Ade nodded in confirmation. Expanding his business to Yaba, Lagos was his uncle's idea. Uncle Kasali had advised that he relocate his company to Nigeria rather than keep enriching the economy of England through the high taxes his company paid the British government. At first, he brushed it off, saying, "At least we can see the benefit of the high taxes," but Uncle Kasali pressed him continuously, suggesting that he at least spread his tentacles to Nigeria if he wouldn't consider relocating.

Jake uttered, "This is your chance, don't fluff it."

"We have a few proposals under consideration from around the world, so just know that this is not cast in stone yet," Tracey chipped in.

Ade was prepared. He had gone over every minute detail before the presentation day and ensured he was well versed in the technicalities that could ruin their venture. He started off confidently, "Yaba, Lagos can be equally matched to Silicon Valley. It is our tech hub, one of a kind and the pride of Africa. The potential of this market is in the billions." His eyes met Tracey's; this time he didn't look away. He continued with his pitch, lifting his chin, spreading his hands when expatiating, and nodding with a slight smile each time he believed he had struck the right notes in the hearts of his investors. He knew so much about technicalities and bureaucracies of the system that could kill any start-up. He recalled how a missing file was the only reason one Mr. Koledowo, a friend of his father, never got his business off the ground.

"But the system is notorious for killing dreams and burying great ideas before twilight," Jake queried.

In a baritone voice Ade muttered, "Yes, it is. So, to make sure this venture stands out, I would like all stakeholders to have the mind-set that we are our own government. That is the only route to success." Jake and Tracey agreed, as they nodded their heads almost at the same time.

The meeting ended after three hours of intense negotiations, and they all came out smiling. Contracts were signed and sealed. Ade felt as if he had a lot to prove. Jake and Tracey had committed much to him and he knew he could not botch it. His mind raced through the list of people to call to break the good news as he headed back to his car. Calling his dad now was not the best idea and his Mom would not be different either. He had no sibling to reach out to. Miriam would have been the best person in this situation. She had a way of celebrating him that made him even happier.

He remembered it was noon on the day he received an email congratulating him as the winner of the National Poetry Competition. He was at his desk composing a poetry piece for Miriam. She was away at the mosque for the Ramadan prayers, praying for him, for her Muslim brethren, for her country Nigeria, and for England. He spread the corners of his lips in a smile and breathed gently as he scribbled words that described her, occasionally stopping to shut his eyes and imagine her face.

Miriam

You're my mirror

My stanza

My rhymes

And everything in between.

Our love knows no religion

Or creed

Through thick or thin

I will be yours.

He was at the door of his apartment waiting for Miriam when she arrived. Before she could say a word to him, she was off the floor in his arms spinning and spinning until she screamed, "Stop please! I'm scared!" He let her down but held on to her tightly, looking into her eyes.

"We won sweetie," he said excitedly.

"What?" She had forgotten about the poetry contest she made him enter eight months ago.

"The National Poetry Competition."

Her ears stood up and her eyes widened. "Oh my goodness!" This time, she lifted herself off the ground and placed her arms around his shoulders, holding on to him and laughing at the same time. With her on him, he moved into his apartment and shut the door behind them.

"I knew you were talented enough to win this prize," she said, looking into his eyes. Then, she placed her lips on his and drew them out. "Gosh! I love you Ade." Miriam's legs were now strapped around his waist, with her butt dancing in his palms as he leaned against the wall. Her breasts warmed his chest.

"I love you too." His breath became heavier and his heartbeat increased, but as soon as he got to the cushion and laid her down, he stopped.

"Why did you stop?" She asked.

"I-I don't know if you want this right now." He was still breathing hard.

"Of course, I do." She pulled him down by the shirt and kissed him again.

Ade could still feel the warmth of those kisses on his lips even now. His head was against the rest of his car seat, recalling that night. The first night they made love to each other. He couldn't handle the frustration of not being able to celebrate his victory with anyone at the moment. Uncle Kasali would have been an option but for the fact that he wouldn't end the call without making huge financial requests. Ade was a money bank to him. A thought crossed his mind. He reached for his pocket and pulled out the blue call card in it.

"Hi."

"This is the man at the elevator earlier today."

"Oh wow… So glad you called."

"Yeah. I was thinking if we could meet up tonight at my apartment."

"Sure. Just text me the address and I'll be there in a jiffy."

As soon as the call dropped, a mild smile settled on Ade's face slowly but the voice of his father in his head cut short the smile. *How many women will you 'sample' before you settle for one?* He brushed the thought off quickly, started the engine of his car and zapped off.

His quarrel with his parents didn't change the way he felt for them. He knew they were right about him settling down with one woman. They always wanted the best for him, and that was the reason they sent him to prestigious schools in Manchester and Cambridge. But as much as they cared, a lot of times, they were overbearing. It was this overbearing attitude that disrupted his love affair with Miriam. But before it did, he had his fair share in messing things up with her.

Miriam was in her red lace underwear in the room of Ade's newly acquired luxury apartment. She was lying beside him watching him flip through some documents in a blue plastic file in preparation for his forthcoming meeting at a tech giant. Her perfectly rounded breasts were bare. He was easily drawn to the breasts of a woman and often prompted her to keep her chest open for him to savour the sight. It was a few days after their graduation and they spent it taking strolls, making love, cooking, eating, and talking poetry. This time, she was talking about her plans, but Ade wasn't listening. She grabbed the paper from his hand, infuriated that she had been talking to an inattentive person.

"What did you say?"

"Really? You weren't listening? Alright then, I should be on my way." She made to leave the bed but he pounced on her playfully and began biting her lips.

"Ouch! You're hurting me. Stop."

"Not until you tell me what you were saying earlier."

"Okay. Fine." Ade stopped and rolled off her, laughing. "I said now that I'm done, I want to pursue my dreams."

"You mean your dreams of becoming a pilot?"

"Sure. My dad promised that if I do well, he would support me in every way he can."

"And if he doesn't?"

"I'll kill him." They exchanged stares and began to laugh until they were out of breath. Silence enveloped the atmosphere suddenly. There were cups on the stools on both sides of the bed with melted chocolate ice cream. Miriam whirled her fingers in the cup by her side and slipped them into Ade's mouth. Ade, who would have resisted for fear of contamination and the many unhygienic consequences he dreaded, licked the liquid around her fingers without hesitation. While he did that, his phone began ringing, but he paid no attention to it. He kept on at her fingers and proceeded to her ear lobes. She turned over to her side so he could properly position himself. Her eyes caught the documents he compiled, and then, his phone. This time, Ade was at her neck. The caller was not giving up and Ade was bent on having a good time. Miriam peeped at the screen to see the caller. *Stranger calling*. Her curiosity was aroused. She pushed Ade aside and pulled herself up. Her face was straight and her neck suddenly grew longer in his eyes.

"Ade pick up this call," she ordered. Ade looked at the screen and immediately took his eyes off. He opened his mouth to say something but she interrupted him. "Pick this call or I walk out on you!" He was hesitant for a while, waiting and hoping that the call would end. When it did, she dialled the number herself and placed it on loudspeaker. Before the call went through, a message came in. *I've missed your touch badly*. Miriam flung her eyes wide and transferred her gaze from the phone to Ade. Without saying a word, she dialled the number again and waited for the receiver. The voice of Chen, the Chinese, came on.

"Hey baby, been calling." She sounded like she was pressed for some lovemaking. Ade lowered his head shamefully.

"You bastard!" Miriam screamed at the top of her voice. Her eyes went watery in an instant and her hands began shaking. Impulsively, she flung the phone at Ade, smashing the side of his face. She jumped off the bed and slipped into her dress which had been lying on the floor. The last thing she expected that day was to find out that her boyfriend was sleeping with her best friend. Ade ran after her as she headed for the door but she slammed it against his face with a loud bang that sent him reversing his steps involuntarily. He blew into the air, jumped up and cussed, embarrassed at himself for not just cheating on the woman he loved dearly but also ruining her friendship with Chen.

The night he ran into Chen, he was at the bar of a club waiting for Miriam. He had been expecting her for over an hour and she was yet to show up. Chen arrived at the bar in a fringe dress that revealed a good portion of her breasts and her entire back. He had never imagined her that pretty in all the times he had seen her. She offered to pay for a glass of alcohol, and then, asked for a dance after Miriam called in to say she wouldn't make it. The music was fast and they swayed their bodies to the rhythm. Moments after, the music became slower and they held each other, moving closer until their lips touched. They didn't stop seeing each other after then, but their meetings were secret until Chen became a bug in his life, asking for sex every now and then. He told her off but she didn't stop. Sometimes, she seduced him with naked pictures of herself and other times, she blackmailed him to get him into her arms again.

Miriam refused to take his calls for weeks and months. She stayed away from his apartment and moved in with her dreadlocked Jamaican friend, Khenan. She spent her days praying on her mat with her beads more than she ever did on normal days. It was as if heartbreak was a call to spirituality. Sometimes, Khenan joked about it, other times, he joined her on the mat and followed her steps even though he was an atheist. It was his way of showing her his support. Meanwhile, Ade was on a desperate search for her. He checked all the places he knew her to visit except Khenan's. He never even knew Khenan existed in her list of friends.

One morning as it rained heavily and he ran into his car to head to work at his new office, he froze, seeing Miriam at the other seat beside him. She was in a black hijab on a short turquoise gown and a pair of pantyhose.

"I have all your keys, remember?" She lifted up her bunch to his face and for a moment, Ade realised that he had given her all access into his entire life that she could easily murder him, if she had the intentions to. She knew his deepest secrets, business plans, and even all his account details and the balance in each of them.

"Miriam," he gasped. He pulled her into his embrace. She shut her eyes tight and whispered in his ears, "It's so hard to stop loving you."

"So hard to stop loving you too," Ade soliloquized. He was standing by the window of his room, watching the rain pour down in torrents. He lifted the wine glass in his hand to the rain and sipped from it afterward. The downpour signified celebration of his victory with Jake and Tracey. He looked behind at the sleeping brown skin beauty lying naked on his bed. Her hair was spread and her hands cupped her breasts to her sides as if trying to lighten their weight. Ade noticed the irritating stretch marks on her butt. He had not seen them when he took off her underwear but now they stared him in the face in their black, zig-zag lines. Miriam had stretch marks too. He had seen them several times and even joked that they were the marks of God on a woman's body. He enjoyed tracing the dark lines with his fingers until she stopped him. But at the sight of the woman on his bed, he couldn't wait for the day to dawn so he could pay her off.

"How dare you offer me money for sex? Do I look like a prostitute?" The brown skin beauty charged at Ade. He was in his bathrobe, sipping a cup of hot water from his mug and getting ready for the new day as well.

"I'm sorry. I thought you were…" he scratched his head, embarrassed at himself for mistaking her for a prostitute.

"If you mistook me for a prostitute because I slipped a call card into your pocket, then, I'm sorry for you." She got up from his bed and cupped her breasts again, this time, shielding her nakedness from him in anger. Her clothes were lying on the floor. She picked them up and threw them on, leaving without a word to him. When she was out of the door, Ade picked up his phone and texted her 'I'm sorry.'

His schedule for the day was too jam-packed for him to find time to pay her an apology visit. He didn't even know her name. He checked the blue call card, where it was written at the top.

Dr. Jennifer Brown

General practitioner, North Manchester General Hospital, Manchester.

He chuckled at the thought that his escapades had led him into the hands of women from different walks of life and occupations. Jennifer was the first doctor on his list and she didn't even look like one. He had always imagined them bespectacled and serious minded. Sometimes, unromantic and highly morally conscious. As he packed his documents together into a suitcase in preparation for his flight to Nigeria in the next twenty-four hours, he received a reply to his text.

Apology accepted. But only because you were great last night.

Slipping out of his bathrobe and into a yellow long sleeve shirt matched with a navy blue blazer, he toyed with the idea of either dating Jennifer to try out what it looks like dating a medical practitioner, or just having her as his fuck buddy. She reminded him of Debbie, his self-acclaimed ex after Miriam and the first and only Igbo girl he ever dated.

Debbie was an investment banker working at one of the top-rated Investment banks in Canary Wharf, London. He met her during the period he was on a scouting spree for angel investors to start New Wave Tech Hub. She came in handy with lots of information on what he should do, where he should go, and who he should meet. Jake Barrow was the first name she had mentioned but added that only luck would enable him to have a one-on-one meeting because nearly every tech hub start-up wanted to pitch their ideas to him. She was the only lady who ticked all the right boxes and came close to Miriam in his fantasy island of beauty, guts, intellect and romance.

On their first formal date, after several meetings at restaurants and parks to discuss funding ideas that could set off his venture, she wore a tight lilac mini dress that revealed her curves and fair legs. Her hair was packed in a bun so high and full, and for the first time, he realised that all the hairdos he had seen on her were her natural hair. He was caught in between telling her how amazing she looked and how much he had fallen in love with her. That night, they clinked glasses, downed deserts, and wrapped it up with several rounds of love making in a hotel room. Her naked back was against Ade as he patted her hair slowly and gently after the last round, looking for the perfect way to communicate what he had in mind.

He tried, "I really don't know how my life would be without you in it," then paused. When she didn't say anything, he continued, "I've not been the same since I met you."

She rolled over to her other side, now facing Ade with her big boobs that he had spent so long fantasizing about until then, and her slightly protruding tummy she tucked in with quality stomach girdles. He had seen the bulge before on one of the days she was in no mood for the discomfort that came with wearing girdles. "Nna… I can't keep up with the too many expectations of women, and the world's beauty standards," she had remarked when she caught his eyes on her stomach area. But this time, Ade's eyes were fixated on her pretty face and naked body lying by his side, hoping for something beautiful to kick-start between them.

"Look, Ade," she began, "I can't do this with you."

"Can't do what, baby?"

"You're a fuck boy, a Yoruba demon. I've seen the way you flirt with pretty women you perceive have some class and style. I've also been let in on your numerous sexual escapades by people whose names I won't mention to you."

Ade got off the bed impulsively and walked to the mirror, placing clenched fists on the mirror stead. He stared at his reflection in search of the demon that Debbie had just described. Then, he transferred his gaze to her reflection. She was no longer lying on her side but seated up now.

"Ade, let's face facts. The best I can be to you is your fuck buddy and I'm fine with that." She wasn't taking her words back. In fact, she had more to say. "Besides, you might someday have plans to relocate to Nigeria and I have no plans to move out of the UK. I can't sacrifice my exceptional career on the altar of love for a **fuck boy**." She emphasized the phrase (fuck boy) so it could ring a bell in his head. Her words landed like a Tyson Fury punch on his jaws. He had nothing to say or do in response except to throw on his clothes and take a walk out of the hotel room.

When he got home, he destroyed all the memories they both shared. He tore the poem he wrote for her and penned a new verse, a one-liner visible on the isolated walls of his room beside the oval size wall clock.

You killed me with your words.

The poem cut a forlorn figure in his exquisite apartment and was a reminder that what goes around sometimes can find their way back to the origin. But for the remaining time, he still had to see Debbie before they stopped communicating, he made sure he initiated dates when he could have a good feel of her in bed. *Since she wants a fuck buddy, I'll show her what the phrase means.*

Ade was on his way out of Future Heir Capital, where he had a conversation with Jake and Tracey in preparation for his journey. He thought about calling Jennifer to fix an evening date but brushed it aside considering being decent for once. A real date wasn't what he wanted but a warm bed for the night and Jennifer would be only a call away. He changed his mind immediately and rather planned a lawn tennis outing with a few of his friends. He was driving out of the premises of Jake's company when Jake called in.

"Would you mind using my private jet for the journey instead?" Jake asked at the other end of the call.

"That's very thoughtful of you but I would kindly decline. You've been nice already," Ade replied.

The call ended quickly and Ade resumed the car engine. He drove to his apartment to catch a rest before changing into his game outfit. Once it was dusk, he grabbed his racket and ball and headed for the court where he met with his friends. They played against one another with Ade beating everyone. He was so good with the game that other people hanging around turned their attention to him and cheered him on. When the game was over, a number of people walked up to him to congratulate him for a skillful play. One of them was Senator Adeyemi. Ade's eyes nearly fell from their sockets on seeing him. He was the father of Oyinkan, an abrasive, narcissist and controlling woman he had dated.

When the pressure of his parents for him to settle down began, he had considered marrying her irrespective of her personality but Senator Adeyemi called for a private meeting with him and dissuaded him from venturing into a marriage everyone knew would definitely fail. Ade had no problems with gutted women but a narcissist and control freak, he wasn't sure he could handle. He still gets baffled that a father could braze up to the truth about his own daughter and save an outsider from her claws.

"Neva niu yu play so we." The accent was familiar to Ade. Senator Adeyemi was notorious for his deep Yoruba accent that glided on every word. Once on national TV, he had said *penkelemesi* instead of *peculiar mess*. And now, he articulated ***never knew you play so well*** like a child just learning to speak the English Language. He wondered whether these Nigerian politicians ever passed verbal reasoning at all. He couldn't imagine that uneducated and semi educated people ruled intellectuals like him in his country.

"We should compete this weekend," the senator proposed once again in his accent.

Ade politely turned down his request with the information that he was embarking on a journey the next day and wouldn't be back in a while. Senator Adeyemi shrugged and shook hands with him before they departed.

Nigeria

NEW WAVE TECH stood boldly at the top of a state of the art office building on Herbert Macaulay Way in the Yaba area of Lagos Mainland. Ade had purchased it for a princely sum after successfully registering the hub with the Corporate Affairs Commission in Nigeria. In order not to have the company's funds wasted, he started by leasing out some floors in the edifice to prospective tenants, since there was no need for the whole structure immediately. New Wave Tech would occupy only the topmost floor at the start. He had also equipped his employees at the Manchester Tech hub well enough to carry out their duties without his overbearing shadow getting in the way.

Now, it was time for him to get some rest before his return to England. He had tried his best to ensure his return journey was inconspicuous. He cautioned his Dad a week before he took off in the air for Nigeria not to let any of the family members get wind of his plans. If they knew their ATM was coming back home, the requests from all and sundry would be so overwhelming that he would have a lot of enemies within the family fold. Extended family members and acquaintances had always burdened him throughout his stay abroad. There was always an issue that needed money to be resolved. It was as if everyone he knew was enmeshed in difficulties and they saw him as the messiah who could solve their problems. It was so bad that he saved Aunty Josephine's number on his phone as Aunty Parasite and Aunty Paulina as Aunty Beggie-Beggie. Uncle Lasisi's name was saved as New Day New Story.

In his shorts and singlet, Ade descended the stairs of his parents' duplex swiftly and headed for the bar. There were wine varieties lined up. He ran his hands through them, as he was not used to his dad's preferences, until he reached a Champagne bottle and stopped at it. He preferred to take the one everyone knew than try out something different due to his fear of allergies. With the bottle in hand accompanied by a wine tumbler in the other, he headed for the living room where his dad was seated watching the mid-day news.

"I haven't said this since you came, but I'm proud of you," his dad said with a lively face. He adored his son so much and was glad to see that the resources he had poured on him didn't go to waste.

"Likewise, I'm proud to have you as my father. Not all fathers would support their son up to Doctorate level with such huge amounts of money."

His father wasn't the super wealthy type. He was just the type that laid out good plans for his family and pursued them until they were achieved. He wanted to have just two children he could give the best to with his resources, unlike the numerous African men who wanted a swarm of kids that they would end up abandoning for their wives to cater for when they can no longer meet up. Ade was his second child after Funke, who died five years after she was born.

Above them, hung on the wall, was the framed poem Ade had scribbled some years back in appreciation for the love and care his parents had shown him. It read:

Parents are sacrificial lambs.

With a ton of buried dreams & shattered hopes

They are heaven's gift

Call them dust. Man. Woo-man

& human.

They toil. Worry. Before they

Recoil into the land where no mortal exists.

"You still have that," Ade nudged at the frame.

"Certainly. I want to keep seeing it until I die."

"Dad, can you just stop this death talk." Ade knew where his father would digress their conversation to. Each time he talked about death, he would slowly change the topic to marriage.

"I can't, son. Your mother and I are getting old. We want to see our grandchildren before our maker calls us home."

"If you want to start this conversation again, Dad, you will leave me no choice than to remind you of how you ruined my relationship with the one woman who, for once, made me comfortable with the idea of marriage."

"What are you talking about, son?"

Ade was talking about the weekend, two and a half years ago, when he flew into Nigeria with Miriam for a special dinner with his parents. He had planned to introduce her as the woman he was to marry. Miriam made him wait till she was through with her aviation school studies, where she trained as a pilot. He seized the opportunity to pursue his Doctorate degree and once she was done, he popped the question.

What was meant to be an innocent statement Miriam made at the dinner ruined the entire relationship. In response to Ade's mother's excitement over being a grandmother in a couple of years, she said, "May Almighty Allah keep you alive to see even your great-grandchildren." There was a sudden silence. Ade's parents exchanged stares at one another and, afterwards, faced him. His mother's lips bent in a downward curve and his father's forehead creased in folds as he lifted his eyes.

"Can I see you privately, son?" His father requested, getting up from his seat and flinging the napkin on his lap to the table. Ade followed him out of the dining room, curious and anxious to know what was going through their minds. Miriam was left with his mother. They looked at each other, one smiling and the other, hiding her sudden displeasure.

"Where's your hijab?" Ade's mother asked.

"I only wear hijabs to the mosque or when I'm observing a spiritual season in my life," Miriam responded and paused, anticipating a friendly explanation for the question but when there was none, she asked, "Why did you ask, Ma'am?"

"No oh… I just thought that as a Muslim, you should be in your hijab." Ade's mother looked away avoiding her stare and further questioning. The smile on Miriam's face gradually dissolved in an inquisitive look. Moments ago, when she walked through the door with Ade, the chubby woman was the nicest person in the world. Now, her tone had changed from nice to one that indicated some level of irritation. While her mind was busy figuring out what had gone wrong, she heard a shout from the upper floor of the duplex.

"Son, you cannot marry a Muslim!" It was Ade's father. He was at the balcony of the first floor of the duplex pacing up and down, angry at his son. He did get angry occasionally but Ade had never witnessed this kind of rage he displayed.

"But I thought you used to say that we're one religion regardless," Ade said with pleading eyes gazing at his father. He was nervous. It showed in the way his voice shook as he spoke. Miriam was the only woman he loved, and hindering their marriage plans meant shattering a part of him.

"We're Christians. She's a Muslim. It's as simple as that!"

"Dad, please, listen to me." Ade was on his knees this time as if his next breath depended on his father's next response. "I have hurt this woman times without number, yet, she forgave me. Who else would love me this much?"

His father turned aside not wanting to be cajoled by his pleading eyes. He inhaled deeply and pressed his lips against one another. Depriving his son of marrying the love of his life was not something he ever imagined he would do but his mind was made up. He took one last look at Ade that meant *Never!* and walked out. Ade screamed, "If you do not allow me to marry Miriam, I would rather die than give you a grandchild."

The voice resounded in the atmosphere to Miriam still in the dining room, alone this time. She sat cold and frozen. This was supposed to be her day. But it didn't look like it at the moment. There was a blurry figure by her side, which her misty eyes did not allow her see in time, but as the tears rolled out of her eyes down her cheeks, she saw him clearly. Ade. He was standing at the entrance of the dining room looking disheartened and defeated. His conversation with his father was loud enough for even the neighbours in the next compound to hear, so he didn't bother explaining what had ensued between them. The tears in her eyes affirmed that she had heard everything.

He walked slowly to her side and took her hand in his. "I'll fight for us," he assured her. But in the months to come, he ended the relationship, telling her he couldn't go against his parents' wish.

Manchester

As Autumn set in, before all the leaves on Manchester's trees fell off and the cold winter nights took centre-stage, Ade stood by the window of his room in his apartment. He was admiring the beautiful rose flowers in his garden which his mother planted when she visited him in Manchester four years ago.

"Whenever you feel alone, let these flowers, when they grow, remind you of how much your father and I love you," she had told him.

These days, he was starting to feel alone. The decision to stay a year without a woman in his bed was starting to take a toll on him. His body vibrated from lack of a feminine touch but his heart ached more from the absence of love. Real love. The kind that Miriam showered on him. The flowers consoled him as they flapped their petals and swayed to the breeze's rhythm. Now, he wished he said a proper goodbye to his parents before leaving Nigeria. His anger at his father for not wanting to accept that disapproving of Miriam had ruined his ability to feel the same way about any other woman had made him book an impromptu flight back to Manchester.

He was glad, anyway, that in a few days, he would be returning to Nigeria to kick off operations at New Wave Tech. It would serve him the opportunity to see his parents again and apologise for 'whisking away' without informing them.

As he perfected plans on his return trip, Jake mentioned to him in passing. "You can use my private jet as a gesture of goodwill as I know the difficulty you have encountered in renting out one for this trip." Ade waved it off and said, "I will travel with a commercial flight, just this time." Although he wished for a private journey- just him and crew members of a private jet- he was trying not to be a burden on Jake but deep down, he knew Jake wouldn't mind. Every journey was a meet and greet with a new woman who ended up in his bed either as a girlfriend or as a fuck buddy. He prayed in his heart that he would have no distractions this time as his personal assistant booked him on a foreign airline to his home country.

Back home, there would be intense sunlight where the trees are green all year round. The season when made in Nigeria goods are celebrated. Ade felt great that he was in good stead to become a major frontrunner in the tech space and flying the '***Made in Nigeria***' kite.

Someday, my boy, you would return home. Uncle Kasali's words to him six years ago. That was poetic and prophetic. Now, he was seated in the luxurious first-class seat set for home. Nigeria. Debbie was right. He had made up his mind to make Nigeria his base and it would have been terrible for her to abandon her fast growing career for his dreams.

The pilots and crew did the courtesies to all travellers who were booked in the first-class cabin. As he listened, he sighted a leggy brown skin lady from a distance in a black cap, white shirt, and a black trousers, the uniform typical of a pilot. She was in a conversation with someone, her back facing him. There was a surge of nervousness that swam through him. He hoped in his heart that it was rather Jennifer, the doctor standing afar off.

But as the brown skin lady turned and began strutting in his direction, his fears were confirmed. He felt his bowels move and his heart freeze for five seconds. This was Miriam. The woman whose heart he shattered several times, yet she forgave him. The woman he couldn't fight for after his father disapproved of her. The woman who disappeared from his life without leaving traces of her whereabouts. This was Miriam.

Her eyes caught his as she drew closer, and she stopped. Her eyes became misty all at once, making it obvious to Ade that she was yet to get over the hurt he and his family had caused her. She had a lot to say but time was against her as she was the one to fly the plane to Nigeria. Ade took in a deep breath as she walked past him but in a split second, she was back at his ear, whispering something to him.

"Six years with you, Ade, and all you did was throw my heart in the bin like I never meant anything." Her voice was shaky and her whisper sounded like something that would have been a yell if not for the immediate environment. Lifting her head away from his, she chided in a sarcastic tone, "I hope you have a jolly ride back home." He was transfixed on a spot, his mouth muted, and his legs felt heavy as if glued to the ground. "This was karma," he thought within.

As soon as the flight took off, he went to empty his bowels that were inflamed because of his encounter with Miriam. He could barely drag himself to the loo. His legs were tired and wobbly, he felt exasperated and out of breath like an athlete who had just finished running a marathon. He remembered once telling Miriam that his life was literally in her hands on realising he had given her access to all information about him and everything he owned before they parted ways. Now, he feared that he was at her mercy. If she was the pilot of the plane, he was definitely going to die.

In the cockpit, Miriam was pervasive, the mere sight of the man who left her hurting gave her goose bumps and a wave of heat permeated through her body. She had always prayed with *a straight face* never to set eyes on him after all he did to her. Now her worst fears metamorphosed right before her very eyes.

Thirty minutes into the flight, the announcement came from a member of the cabin crew that the pilot took ill and had to excuse herself from flying the aeroplane. So, the newbie first officer who had less than one thousand flying hours under his belt had to take charge of the flight.

"We will now commence our descent. The time is seven-thirty pm in Lagos with a temperature of twenty-three degrees celsius," the first officer announced from the cockpit as he prepared the passengers for landing. "Flight attendants, prepare for landing please." There was a minute pause and then, the baritone voice echoed from the speakers dotted inside the plane, "Cabin crew, please take your seats for landing." Ade was super excited at the prospect of landing in one piece. It had been a long and traumatic journey but the sequence of events with Miriam excusing herself from flying was the perfect outcome for him. As he was reminiscing on what might have been, there was a thud, a loud bang. Thick smoke enveloped the aeroplane and the noise of blaring sirens rended the air with emergency services in tow.

The major newspaper headlines the next morning read: *aircraft crash-lands in Lagos, seven passengers dead, several injured*.

A week later, the remains of Ade Olanihun were interred at the upscale cemetery where only the wealthy began their journey home. A tall leggy brown skin lady in crutches, sporting dark glasses was in the crowd to pay her last respects. As the priest made the sign of the cross and opened his mouth to say "Rest in peace," she voiced silently along.

"Rest in pieces."

TROUBLE IN UMUDIKE

There was tranquility in the Umudike community area in Ikwuano, as people gathered round the television set in Mazi Okafor's compound to listen to the 9 pm news. While the news broadcast was ongoing, grave silence enveloped the room as everyone waited for Mazi to relay the news back to them. Mazi was the only resident in the community that spoke Queens English, and he used this to maximum benefit. He had a charm about him and carried himself with the utmost dignity and panache, knowing that he was very much respected within the community and basks in the euphoria of his status. He wore the news on his face like cinema guests watching a horror movie. Chinedu Okafor, the son of his elder brother, has brought disrepute to the Umudike Community, and this was an abomination of monumental proportions.

As the newscaster drew the curtains on the news for the night, Mazi Okafor started pacing around the room, in a swift manner. Chinedu had always been hot-headed, but he never knew he could have disrespected his father this way. Mazi Okafor began to strategize on how he would break the news to the gathering crowd who were fidgeting and growing restless. It was the norm to have the whole village gather to listen to the news at Mazi's residence and the villagers would analyse the news for hours unending once Mazi had relayed the major headlines back to them.

His lack of communication with them since the news broadcast came to a halt gave way to intense apprehensions and wailing by some bystanders. How would I break this news to them? Do I tell them the whole story that would spark a mourning of sorts or do I cover this up to a more appropriate time? He needed time to think this through and come up with a tactical response. His face wore the colour of sorrow, dark with a hint of grey. Today is not the day to adorn this community with the garment of mourning, he spoke to no one in particular. A bystander Ifeanyi replied "Mazi, permit us to drown in our sorrow tonight, don't delay." Mazi was evasive and pretended not to hear him.

Only Mazi Okafor knew of the deep agony that claimed the life of his brother's wife. As he was lost in thought, his mind raced to the events of the last few years and the sea of problems Chinedu had caused the family. His brother Odogwu, as he was fondly called, was responsible for his claim to literacy and was the only surviving parent of Chinedu, Chidi and Chike, childbirth complications meant the boys were motherless and their father took up the lone responsibility of bringing up his sons till they reached adulthood. Mazi had pressured Odogwu; it was time to end the grief and find a companion who would help him lessen his burden.

He had married Uzoamaka, who was untainted by any stain, in a small ceremony to preserve the memory of his late wife. On the night of the traditional ceremony, he had received a telephone call that soured his mood, his containers had landed at the seaports in Lagos. Wrong timing, he yelped stamping his feet on the hardwood flooring. "Odogwu hope no problem," she said with concern written on her face. By now she was scantily dressed, as she was ready to end her long wait for sex and savour the excitement of womanhood. "Uzzy, there's a problem," his clothes are now off the deck. Even the sound of Uzzy as he would call her to soften her sounded flat as his words escaped into thin air. "I have to supervise the unloading of my consignment that just landed. The last time the containers arrived at the ports without my direct supervision, most of the goods developed wings."

He flapped his hands intermittently as if he wanted to fly. "Finger pointing between port officials and my boys never resolved the matter." Grave silence enveloped the room as Odogwu's actions left her sorrowful.

As Odogwu made way to leave the house with Chidi and Chike, he called out to Chinedu, his first son who sat his West Africa Senior Certificate exams around the same time as his new bride. Chinedu always wondered why his father had to marry a lady young enough to be his daughter. His father's voice woke him up from his thoughts, "I will be travelling out-of-town tonight with your brothers," he said. Chinedu glanced first at his watch before he glanced at his father's face, he uttered nothing, he was unbothered to throw his father's words back at him that only vagabonds leave the sanctity of their home at the dead of the night. Odogwu continued slowly as if delivering the words in bitesize would pass his message across the right way. He said, "make sure you behave yourself and look after my wife, I don't want to hear any tales of misdemeanour," he charged in a stern voice.

Chinedu replied disinterested, "Papa, you can take her with you as Uzoamaka isn't a child that requires any special attention." His fears were valid; he always doubted Chinedu was his biological son, his dodgy character traits always made him question his paternity, if not how could he call my Uzzy by her first name. The other two boys were a splitting image of him, and he had a soft spot for them, and showed them the intricacies of his business to place them in good stead once the inevitable happened. They were the only ones who could sign invoices and authorise payments whenever he was away on his numerous trips.

It was as if Chinedu could read his father's mind, "I wish you a safe journey Papa, drive safe sir". He enthused emphatically as if desperate to be rid of them. Uzoamaka was sorrowful, this was supposed to be the night her new husband would thrust her from earth to heaven and then back to earth. She had planned the sequence of her moans. How she would bite her lips and lose herself in reckless abandon when Odogwu, her Odogwu pounded her intensely with youthful vigour. She had allowed the thoughts of him being old enough to be her *father* escape her mind, she would just enjoy it and put the whole of her being into the marriage to make it work.

She had planned to call her elder sister Onyinye in the morning, who had always taunted her for keeping her virtue till marriage, after enjoying a great night of sex. But Odogwu was nowhere to be found. Maybe he valued his business more than he valued me, and there is a possibility I am not his dream woman, she voiced out aloud with a hint of regret in her voice.

Her joy was to keep herself till her wedding night, which she had done gracefully despite the number of men who were desperate to move heaven and earth to get in between her legs. She was passionate and adamant about the life she wanted to live. She had known Chinedu and his brothers since elementary school days and had shared an intense kiss with Chinedu in High School long before her father proposed that she filled the void in Odogwu's life. It's been eighteen long years since Odogwu lost his wife, who was pivotal to his business success, and they all felt the timing was right for him to re-marry. Somehow, he needed to fill the void and stop living in isolation and Uzoamaka was deemed the perfect choice to make this happen.

Uzoamaka and Chinedu had a burning flame since their teenage years. In the naivety of that age they had pierced fingers, matched blood drowning in innocence with a vow to marry each other. However their plan was soured by her Father who was more interested in the *"**Kolanut**"* and the other custom gifts that would make him a tad richer.

That night as Odogwu zoomed off in his White Range Rover SUV, Chinedu couldn't believe his luck, his teenage love left under the same roof with him. He buried the thoughts as soon as it flashed through his mind "*she is now my father's companion*" it would be a taboo, an abomination of great proportions for me to do this, he chided himself. 'How stupid of me to think I can drink from the same 'well' as father?' As his mind held him in captivity, Uzoamaka walked past in her nightgown; he could see her glory from the silk nightie that showed her in complete splendour hiding nothing to the imagination. Her buttocks were rotund and her two breasts stood at attention. Her curves had grown so big and the more Chinedu rested his eyes on her bosom, the more his body burnt intensely.

'Did father set a trap for me?' His inner mind questioned his senses that had stopped functioning in the correct manner. He was supposed to be the heir apparent to his flourishing business and here he was about to lose everything all because he lacked self-control, he thought within. He avoided Uzoamaka like a plague the first three weeks after Odogwu left home. On the night that made it exactly four weeks after Odogwu left home, under the canopy of darkness—they bumped into each other by accident as he made way to put on the generator as the Power Holding Company acted true to their name, 'they held the light as was now customary.'

Uzoamaka said "Why have you been avoiding me young man?" Rolling her eyes. Chinedu was shell-shocked, he couldn't utter a word and his body became stiff. He thought within 'this must be a devil in human form who is hell bent on wrecking his claim to his father's wealth.' The whole event felt like a bad dream to him. She buried herself in his embrace forcefully letting out a little moan.

At that point, his resistance crumbled. As darkness pervaded the whole house, it was as if amadioha consciously orchestrated Chinedu's downfall. The sequence of events that followed that night were dark and grim. Chinedu had deflowered his father's new wife; he had trodden the paths where no one dared, as he began to wear his trousers, he noticed Uzoamaka was turning blue and pale. The beam and sheer joy in her eyes while they romped on her matrimonial bed had long disappeared. Uzoamaka frantically began to lose her breath, her chest tightening, followed by excruciating pain.

"Give me water, I'm running out of breath," she said faintly. Chinedu, panting heavily, ran to the kitchen, where he reached for the ten litres container filled with water. Overwhelmed with confusion, he spilled half of the water and nearly tripped himself as he made haste to revive Uzoamaka. Upon his return, Uzoamaka laid on the bed lifeless. He emptied the container of water on her face, shaking her vigorously. He could only hear his own voice as he screamed into her left ear. Everywhere was dead silent.

The thrusting that night was fierce, till she withered into oblivion.

He ran to the living room and picked up the wired telephone that was a sign of the prestigious life they lived. The wired telephone always gathered dust as it was for Odogwu's exclusive use. He always whispered into it not wanting anyone to eavesdrop into his business dealings with his Oyinbo partners. Fidgeting, he made a call to Mazi his Uncle, "Mazi, there is fire on the mountain, Uzoamaka is dead." Mazi replied "Tufiakwa," tell me this is a bad joke."

"Uncle, I wish it was, I seriously wish it was," Chinedu said sobbing. Then there was an awkward silence before the line went dead.

Mazi was exasperated; he made frantic calls to his brother. The phone rang with no response. This was more than he had bargained for, Odogwu becoming a widower for the second time was hard to decipher. Before nightfall, Odogwu returned Mazi's call.

"Hello Mazi, hope no problem," he said in high spirits. The weight of the tragedy bore hard on Mazi. "There is a problem, major problem. Where are you?" Mazi asked. "I have been in Lagos for some time now," Odogwu said now agitated. "Can I come and see you for an urgent matter?" Mazi asked. Odogwu replied, "It won't be possible to see me until another two weeks. Whatever the matter is, say it over the phone."

He always said that after the *death* of his first wife, he had the strength of character to withstand any news, no matter how bad.

Mazi finding immense courage whispered, "Uzoamaka is dead, cause of death unknown, but I'm still digging for more information." Odogwu yelled "WHAT! Not my Uzoamaka. Not my Uzzy," he continued, his teary voice tugging at Mazi's heart.

Mazi consoled him "Ndo, take heart, we shall get to the root of this matter."

The shock of the news Odogwu had just received was too much to bear. He fell in a heap and had to be consoled by Chidi and Chike. That night Odogwu with his sons returned home, the journey was an unusual one. Whenever they travelled, Odogwu would normally tell them folklore stories that always made Chidi and Chike reel in laughter, but this trip was different. They both grieved with their father and even as they felt the pangs of hunger, they could not muster the courage to tell their father to stop at their favorite bush meat and palm wine joint.

This was a double tragedy to Uzoamaka's parents, who buried their first son eighteen months ago. The news of Uzoamaka's death soon hit the streets. The new bride with the world at her feet was dead, and the cause of her death was shrouded in secrecy. This is the kind of news that was shared hush-hush; it was an abomination. The night Chinedu was intimate with Uzoamaka, the walls creaked, leaving gaping holes. Uzoamaka's fiery noise from the bedroom escaped into thin air and leaked into the ears of Rosemary, their housemaid. As Chinedu disappeared into the night as he tried to clean up his mess, Rosemary tiptoed into the room where Uzoamaka's still body lay. She emptied the jewelry box and disappeared into the night.

Chinedu came back home and the backdoor which was left unlocked raised his suspicions. "Rosemary! Rosemary," he called out. Grave silence enveloped the house. He went to her room and saw that the whole place was empty save for her unfinished dinner.

He ran back to the room where Uzoamaka's body lay and deep-cleaned the stain that hung precariously on the rumpled sheets. Chinedu was trembling as his hands brushed Uzoamaka's face unknowingly. The more he stayed in the room to wipe out every trace of his involvement, his heart continued to race at the sound of honking cars plying the main road. The noise from neighbours going about their normal activities and unfamiliar voices sounded like his father.

Odogwu arrived home with the boys as Chinedu stayed awake, his encounter with Uzoamaka left his heart racing. What happened? Where is Uzoamaka? Was she sleeping? Why is the backdoor unlocked? Chinedu was befuddled and didn't know where to start.

I came home to see that Rosemary was nowhere to be found.

Odogwu uttered no words, picked his car keys and stormed out of the house in rage. He arrived the house of Eze-Alusi the Chief Priest and slammed his car door as he dashed into the shrine. Eze-Alusi looked bewildered as he saw him, "hope all is well Odogwu?"

"Uzoamaka is dead and whoever has done this must pay for this," Odogwu said with bloodshot eyes and his words incoherent.

Eze Alusi was stunned and without prompt dashed into the inner shrine and began to invoke the gods to punish whoever killed Uzoamaka. He came out his face beaming with delight, "Amadioha will take care of the rest. Go Odogwu, the gods will do the rest."

"Ise," said Odogwu as he passed a small envelope to the Chief Priest.

A week after, Odogwu buried Uzoamaka in a quiet ceremony. To preserve her memory, he had promised not to marry any other woman. The indignation of burying two wives made him sorrowful for months unending. As his sons chose their path and left home, he saw no reason to marry a third wife. Most of the nights when he slept, he would see Uzoamaka appear to him saying only one sentence, 'the hidden secrets will someday be revealed,' before she vanished. He was haunted by nightfall and this made him frail. His hair had become white and his bulky frame now resembled a withering plant. His thriving business had since turned south, and he spent most days in between hospital appointments. The effect of the latest tragedy was more than telling.

Five years later, Chinedu's wife Nneka has had seven pregnancies, none passes the third month before she miscarries. Her colourful smile in the early years of their marriage was no more. She looked weary from the trauma of her womb being labelled a home for lifeless babies. She began to seek a spiritual solution. Chinedu always pacified her with calming words, but it no longer worked for her. She attended a three day crusade at the Mountain of Fire and Miracles Ministry in Onitsha. The pastor spoke to her in whispers, "the Lord said, 'there is blood on your husband's hands' until he apologises there won't be any reprieve for you."

A week after the crusade ended, she wakes him up at the dead of the night, sobbing. "Please let's apologise to whoever you have offended to have mercy on you, on me, on us," she mumbled the words.

"Ebe, I know this is tough, but let's do this for our unborn children," Nneka continued.

"Go back to sleep Nnc. We will talk about this in the morning," Chinedu replied half-asleep.

The next week, Chinedu goes to confess with the family elders and his brothers present.

"I have a confession," Chinedu said looking perplexed, his knees sunk into the sand in his father's courtyard. His wife Nneka beside him as they both wore a pitiful look. "I have offended father greatly," he continued. Udofia, his Uncle, spoke next cutting him short "there is nothing coming from the heaven that the earth cannot receive. Tell us, we are the only ones who can placate your father. *Gidi gidi bụ ugwu eze*," he said.

"I slept with Uzoamaka my father's bride that night she passed away, but she made the first move," Chinedu said looking burnt. Chants of Tufia rented the air with some elders pacifying Odogwu who was mouthing expletives at his first son. "Uzoamaka was my first love right from secondary school days, we had promised each other marriage," Chinedu continued.

"Save us the gory details," Aunty Chibundu said her wrapper now on the floor. Uncle Livinus spoke next and mentioned that this was a great tragedy which they must all reason together to resolve. Chidi and Chike fixed their eyes on the ground, both still in shock from the news they just heard.

"Forgive me Odogwu, I have erred greatly. Forgive me for my misdemeanour," Chinedu pleaded his eyes crowded with tears. Odogwu stormed inside burning with rage, he came out with his cutlass that sliced through the mango tree last week.

Before Chinedu could sense what was happening, Odogwu thrust the cutlass into his neck as his blood splattered on the front yard.

For the second time, tragedy walked through their front door majestic. Odogwu had snuffed the life out of Chinedu. Violence came before dusk and left a deadly mark on Odogwu's abode. The police came and whisked Odogwu behind bars with the news on the network news.

As Mazi Okafor reflected on the tragedy that has turned his brother's home into a house of mourning, he burst into a torrent of tears and the whole village joined him in wailing. They cried tears until the heavens opened and a heavy downpour washed away their tears. Mazi Okafor still in shock said, "may this be the end of our sorrow."

BLINDED BY SILENCE

FAUSAT

She looked dishevelled and malnourished. She had been married to Umaru for over seven years, but they had caressed poverty for the greater part of their Union. The first day she met Umaru, she was held hostage by excitement, and let her guard down as her desire to exit her father's house before the constant reminders about her waning years would hold her tight by the jugular, clouding sound judgement. Her father was a Lieutenant Colonel in the Nigerian army who had five wives, and her mother was the only one that ate rice without chicken with him in a beleaguered face me, I face you apartment. She could have been the only one if he hadn't found comfort in the beds of strange women. She had witnessed first-hand the morning dew and hailstorm any matrimony could present.

In the early years of their marriage, when her father remained in Kaduna, their home had excitement in different shades and her bed was warm. But when her father was posted to Port Harcourt, Jos, Maiduguri and Sokoto all within the space of five dark years, as her mother would say anytime she told the story that turned her eyes into a flood of tears.

She painted those five years of doom, in gloom and perpetual sorrow.

"Fausat my daughter, never marry a man like your father," Mother would say with a lump forming in her throat and a croaky voice. "But Mama, our culture allows a man to marry as many women as he wants. And at least father has shown you enough respect by not bringing any of his concubines' home." She would reply to her mother, drowned in innocence. Mother would look at her and shake her head in pity with a look that bemoaned her naivety, rolling her eyes to perfection.

MOTHER (Mrs Binta Raji)

She didn't think her daughter understood men and the ways their hungry mind worked. Every work posting birthed a new mistress and unrelenting anguish. Her bed became lonely and grief pervaded her whole essence as if mourning the demise of her once happy union. In her frustration, she barged into the office of the General Officer Commanding the 1 Division Kaduna, unannounced accusing him of breaking up her once happy home. "If only you didn't post him out of Kaduna," she barked at the G.O.C. Grave silence enveloped the atmosphere as the G.O.C looked perplexed at her effrontery to storm into his office uninvited. A minute later he charged at his personal secretary, and sent for Lt. Col Raji. "He needs to report here tonight."

"YES SIR," the secretary replied, giving full military honours in cognisance that his boss had been deeply wounded. Binta became very apprehensive as tensions in the room were pitch high. She thought within 'no one battles with a soldier without bearing the brunt, talk-less of sparring with a high-ranking officer.'

After five long hours, Lt. Col Raji arrived looking drained. On his way to Kaduna, he had made frantic calls to some colleagues within his inner circle to gain more perspective on the reason for his recall, but no one gave him a clue. As soon as he stepped into the G.O.C's office, he could sense the palpable tension in the room. The G.O.C spoke showing no emotion, "your wife affronted constituted authority earlier today." This has never happened in the history of this division. Lt. Col Raji's eyes became smoky red and his face sullen "Sir, you mean she insulted you?" he asked in a tone that reeked of unbelief. The G.O.C spoke for one last time with fiery eyes, "here's my verdict, your wife must leave the barracks tonight, never to return." "Yes sir," he echoed tamely.

That night was the last she spent within the barracks and aided her well-earned moniker, 'the untamed wife of Lt. Col Raji.' The scar of her misdemeanour would follow her boldly to the graveyard.

FAUSAT

BANTERS WERE THROWN her way in the barracks, where two or three gathered the misdemeanour of mother became a worthy news story- Lt. Col Raji's wife smothered the G.O.C and many more tales were conjured by those who found joy in spreading false information.

As soon as mother left, her footprints were washed away from their large compound, by father's four wives who filled the vacuum created after Father was reposted to 1 Division Kaduna by the G.O.C. It was as if the G.O.C was taunting her mother, now that he is back home, you still can't have him. See what your lack of manners for constituted authority has caused you, the strange voice fiddling with her imaginations would concoct that line. All traces of mother were wiped away with speed as if she was never married to father. Her wedding picture, that was notable in the living room, had become a distant memory as a black coloured wall clock now occupied that space with aplomb. There were days father's troublesome wives threw tantrums her way. Ugochi, the former Portharcourt *runs-girl* who father met at the drinking joint in Bori Camp, always had an abundance of squabbles in her locker room. There was a day they were engaged in a brawl spilling the soup over the pristine cooking gas and the immaculate kitchen tiles. That night, as soon as Ugochi saw father, she wept uncontrollably, finding the courage to speak after he held her in a warm embrace. "This house cannot contain me and this mannerless girl, like mother, like daughter."Ugochi said fuming. Father scrutinised me with great intent and said, "the next time you misbehave in this house, your mother will have a companion wherever she is."

"It won't happen again SIR," she said, her eyes fixed on the ground.

"It better not," Father replied, storming into the hallway, Ugochi on his tail.

On the first day that she found Cupid, her path crossed with Umaru. She later found out he was a successful farmer, at the Sheikh Abubakar Gumi Central market, Kaduna. She was supposed to be running errands for her father, but she was here in the company of a man who locked her in his gaze, professing his desires. She was savouring the attention to full tilt. Umaru asked with an air of confidence, "would you be my wife?" She was shocked. Even though the atmosphere was clouded by love, she mustered some inner strength and yelled back at him, "give me my due respect, true love isn't like a cheap perfume."

He wore a smile that echoed, "stop playing hard to get. Let's get straight to the crux of the matter, on first sight, your love serenades my heart," he enthused, his face breaking into a beam. The breeze was cool against their skin, as if in agreement with Umaru. He placed his hands on her slim waist, drawing her closer to him. She avoided his gaze as her heart thumped against her chest. She was flustered and a little overwhelmed by his open declaration of his love for her. She had never felt anything like this before.

"Will you marry me?" he asked again, solemnly, his forefinger drawing circles on her bare shoulders. Her nipples tightened at his touch.

"Yes. Yes, I will marry you," she blurted, embarrassed that this fairly strange man she just agreed to marry would think she was cheap, easy to win over. Her mother would have her head on a round plate if she ever found out.

The economy of the Country continued to nosedive, and the people continue their speedy descent into the abyss of poverty at an alarming rate. The new president who had promised heaven on earth was only as good in the realm of false promises.

Five children in seven years, meant they had opened the doors wide to poverty, and its embrace so warm, indicated they were in this for the long haul. Fausat always told Umaru he needed to be a MAN after his catastrophic fall from grace and fend for the family after they had their second child, but he knew her weakness and capitalised on it to great effect. His touch sent her defence mechanisms flying into thin air and after each night of intense lovemaking her protruding belly weeks after would signal that just one night of lovemaking is all that is needed.

Umaru's insatiable appetite for sex clouded his imagination that his manhood should be under lock and key till he could fend for the family and stop sowing seeds that would bring offspring to the world he couldn't afford to cater for. The last time they had a furious exchange, it ended up being a community fight. She said *I do* to Umaru at the marketplace, where hagglers bargain over food prices, little wonder their dark secrets has found its way to the market stalls. The working-class women on their street wonder why she couldn't close her parting legs to a man who had conveniently turned her into a child-bearing factory. She was unmoved by their taunts, some of their other neighbours had as many as twelve children and she couldn't say what they did for a living.

UMARU

He married Fausat as a successful farmer with over twenty hectares of land in Kajuru with lush harvests and the produce sold to the south. The land was bequeathed to him by his late grandfather with his late father to tend it until he could navigate his way through the complexities of life. His life became darkened after General Sani became president, the former military dictator who forgot his prized possessions in the seat of power which he so desperately craved to retrieve. The president was their kin and kindred, he grew up in the town next to theirs, so they threw all they had into the ring to support him.

Calamity came through the back door one fateful morning when rampaging herdsmen destroyed his farmland and gunned down everyone at sight in cold blood. Blood stains kissed the earth and the ground quakes in disgust. Fausat came to him agitated, "Umaru, you need to use your connections to get this matter to the press. Let's seek justice and bring the bad guys to account for their misdemeanour and the government needs to be aware of their failings so they can beef up security as required." He consoled her with a warm embrace and replied sheepishly, "General Sani is one of us, this is tantamount to us bringing down his government." He gestured at her with his eyes, pleading. Fausat was enraged, "have you been hypnotised like your brother Ibrahim who lost all he had to the menace of Boko haram but preferred to remain mute because of General Sani? Does General Sani even know you? Does he understand your pain and suffering?" She continued with her anger heating up the whole house. He soothed her frayed nerves with renewed hope, even though he was drenched in sweat, when there is life, there is hope. He sounded like a man beaten to a pulp but who was feigning some non-existent magical strength.

General Sani, the brother who the southern divide had coloured with a garment of nepotism, ethnocentrism and bigotry and who true to type has brought untold hardship, hunger and anger in great proportion to the nation. The land has been ravaged by the inferno of silence, the general hates to hear the chorus of dissenting voices. The secret police and the anti-corruption agencies have been well equipped to deal with and muscle any egghead who wants to be a clog in the wheel of their moving train. From Kaduna to Kano and Katsina, day by day the once vocal elders have all lost their vocal cords. Their fluffy cheeks stained from wet kisses and their once vociferous attacks on the previous government has faded into the dark skies. Fausat was visibly furious by his stupidity, a thriving business that had lasted three generations was going extinct and he folded his arms aloof, sinking under the weight of tribalism.

After another attack in their adjoining community, Fausat cried all through the night, "Umaru, why are you doing this to yourself?" He could sense she was on fire. "Why can't you speak up against the failings of your kinsman?" she snapped in no direction. "You can't understand the complexities involved," he responded with guilt written all over his face. Deep down he knew he should speak out, he had lost so much, and he continued to lose his sanity and all the knots that tie his humanity together. He is in deep agony and still finds a way to conjure a smile, however he brainwashed himself to believe he was fighting a worthy cause for his kindred. They were taught to be united in all seasons, wealth and poverty, hence his unbridled loyalty. Uncle Shehu, who spoke against the establishment, has been thrown in the big house, he was once a favourite of the powers that be.

FAUSAT

At the start of the harmattan season, Umaru came home with a strange woman. Her breasts were firm and pointed, which resonated her age. Her skin was ripened like fresh plantain.

Fausat seething with rage asked, "Umaru, don't tell me you're bringing home another woman to join us in this state of penury?" Looking at the pile of bags on the doorway. She continued, "Have you forgotten you live on support from your kin and kindred?"

Umaru was evasive, avoiding eye contact. When he found his voice, he said abrasively, "all I have done was for your benefit, seeing you have five children to cater for, I felt Maryam would ease your burden." In a moment, Fausat remembered her words to her mother, she yelled out, "NO! No, this can't be me." She walked to the room in haste. By now Maryam had used Umaru as a shield, her small frame taking cover behind his bulky figure. He whispered to Maryam, "you have nothing to fear." Umaru began to scream at the top of his voice, "you either stay or leave, Maryam is here to stay."

His words weakened her resolve and she became cold like melting ice. She knew she had lost the WAR.

BIO

Tolu' Akinyemi is an exceptional talent and an out-of-the box creative thinker; a change management agent and a leader par excellence. Tolu' is a business analyst and financial crime consultant as well as a Certified Anti-Money Laundering Specialist (CAMS) with extensive experience working with leading Investment Banks and Consultancy Firms. Tolu' is also a personal development and career coach and a prolific writer with more than 10 years' writing experience. He is a mentor to hundreds of young people. He worked as an Associate Mentor in St Mary's School, Cheshunt and as an Inclusion Mentor at Barnwell School, Stevenage in the United Kingdom, helping students raise their aspirations and standards of performance and helping them cope with transitions from one educational stage to another.

A man whom many refer to as "Mr Vision," he is a trained economist from Ekiti State University, formerly known as University of Ado-Ekiti (UNAD). He sat his Masters' Degree in

Accounting and Financial Management at the University of Hertfordshire, Hatfield, United Kingdom. Tolu' was a student ambassador at the University of Hertfordshire, Hatfield, representing the University in major forums and engaging with young people during various assignments.

Tolu' Akinyemi is a home-grown talent; an alumnus of the Daystar Leadership Academy (DLA). He is passionate about people and wealth creation. He believes strongly that life is about impacting others. In his words, "To have a secure future, we must be willing to pay the price in order to earn the prize."

Tolu' has headlined and featured in various Open Slam, Poetry Slam, Spoken Word, and Open Mic events in and outside the United Kingdom. He also inspires large audiences through spoken word performances, he has appeared as a keynote speaker in major forums and events, and he facilitates creative writing master classes to all types of audiences.

Tolu' Akinyemi was born in Ado-Ekiti, Nigeria and currently lives in the United Kingdom. Tolu' is an ardent supporter of Chelsea Football Club, London.

You can connect with Tolu' on his various Social Media

Accounts:

Instagram: @ToluToludo

Facebook: facebook.com/toluaakinyemi

Twitter: @ToluAkinyemi

AUTHOR'S NOTE

Thank you for the time you have taken to read this book. I do hope you enjoyed the stories in it.

If you loved the book and have a minute to spare, I would really appreciate a short review on the page or site where you bought the book. Your help in spreading the word is greatly appreciated. Reviews from readers like you make a huge difference in helping new readers decide to get the book.

Thank you!

Tolu' Akinyemi

DEAD CATS
DON'T MEOW
Don't waste the ninth life.
A COLLECTION OF POETIC WISDOM FOR THE DISCERNING
(SERIES 3)
TOLU' A. AKINYEMI

NEVER PLAY
GAMES WITH
THE DEVIL
TOLU' A. AKINYEMI

FROM THE AUTHOR OF
DEAD LIONS DON'T ROAR AND
UNRAVEL YOUR HIDDEN GEMS
DEAD DOGS
DON'T BARK
...And they don't bite.
A COLLECTION OF POETIC WISDOM FOR THE DISCERNING
(SERIES 2)
TOLU' A. AKINYEMI

FROM THE AUTHOR OF 'DEAD
LIONS DON'T ROAR'
UNRAVEL
YOUR
HIDDEN
GEMS
A COLLECTION OF
INSPIRATIONAL
AND MOTIVATIONAL
ESSAYS
TOLU' A. AKINYEMI